J CAS
Casanova, Mary.
The klipfish code

W9-AVM-320

AVON PUBLIC LIBRARY
BOX 977/200 BENCHMARK RD
AVON, CO 81620

EAGLE VALLEY LIBRARY DISTRICT

1 06 0004348963

# The
# Klipfish Code

# The Klipfish Code

by
Mary Casanova

HOUGHTON MIFFLIN COMPANY
BOSTON 2007

AVON PUBLIC LIBRARY
BOX 977 / 200 BENCHMARK RD
AVON, CO 81620

Text copyright © 2007 by Mary Casanova

Maps by Stephanie M. Cooper

All rights reserved. For information about permission to reproduce
selections from this book, write to Permissions, Houghton Mifflin Company,
215 Park Avenue South, New York, New York 10003.

www.houghtonmifflinbooks.com

The text of this book is set in ITC Legacy Serif.

*Library of Congress Cataloging-in-Publication Data*
Casanova, Mary.
The klipfish code / by Mary Casanova.
p. cm.
Summary: Sent with her younger brother to Godøy Island to live with her aunt and
grandfather after Germans bomb Norway in 1940, ten-year-old Merit longs to join her
parents in the Resistance and when her aunt, a teacher, is taken away two years later,
she resents even more the Nazis' presence and her grandfather's refusal to oppose
them. Includes historical facts and glossary.
Includes bibliographical references.
ISBN-13: 978-0-618-88393-6 (hardcover)
ISBN-10: 0-618-88393-2 (hardcover)
1. Norway—History—German occupation, 1940-1945—Juvenile fiction. [1. Norway—
History—German occupation, 1940-1945—Fiction. 2. Patriotism—Fiction. 3. Family
life—Norway—Fiction. 4. Refugees—Fiction. 5. World War, 1939-1945—Underground
movements—Norway—Fiction.] I. Title.
PZ7.C266Kli 2007
[Fic]—dc22
2007012752
Manufactured in the United States of America
MP 10 9 8 7 6 5 4 3

AVON PUBLIC LIBRARY
BOX 977/200 BENCHMARK RD.
AVON, CO 81620

*For my friend Johanne Moe,*
*who grew up in Norway*
*during World War II*

## ACKNOWLEDGMENTS

Many thanks to my editor, Ann Rider, who believed in this story, asked questions to stretch me further as a writer, and helped bring this story to fruition. *Tusen takk!* Our Norwegian ancestors would be proud of us.

No manuscript is complete without the fingerprints and feedback of others, including my family—Charlie, Kate, and Eric Casanova—as well as Hannah Riesgraf, Joyce Gazelka, Susan Gazelka, Lise Lunge-Larsen, Faythe Thureen, Johanne Moe, Tamara England, Mark Speltz, Mary and Andy Anderson, Huns and Marlene Wagner, Jim Hanson, and Hannah Heibel. And as always, a thanks to my local writers' group: Karen Severson, Sheryl Peterson, Shawn Shofner, Lynn Naeckel, Kate Miller, and Jessi-Lyn Curry; and the Oberholtzer Foundation, which has supported meeting on Mallard Island with writers Jane Resh Thomas, Cindy Rogers, Kitty Baker, Maryann Weidt, Phyllis Root, Alice Duggan, Lois Berg, Barb Santucci, Marsha Chall, Catherine Friend, and Janet Lawson.

A special thanks to the staff and curators at the Norwegian Resistance Museums in Oslo, Ålesund, and Godøy Island and for carefully documenting this period in history.

Finally, a heart full of thanks to Eric and Charlie for traveling with me to Norway to find Marit's story.

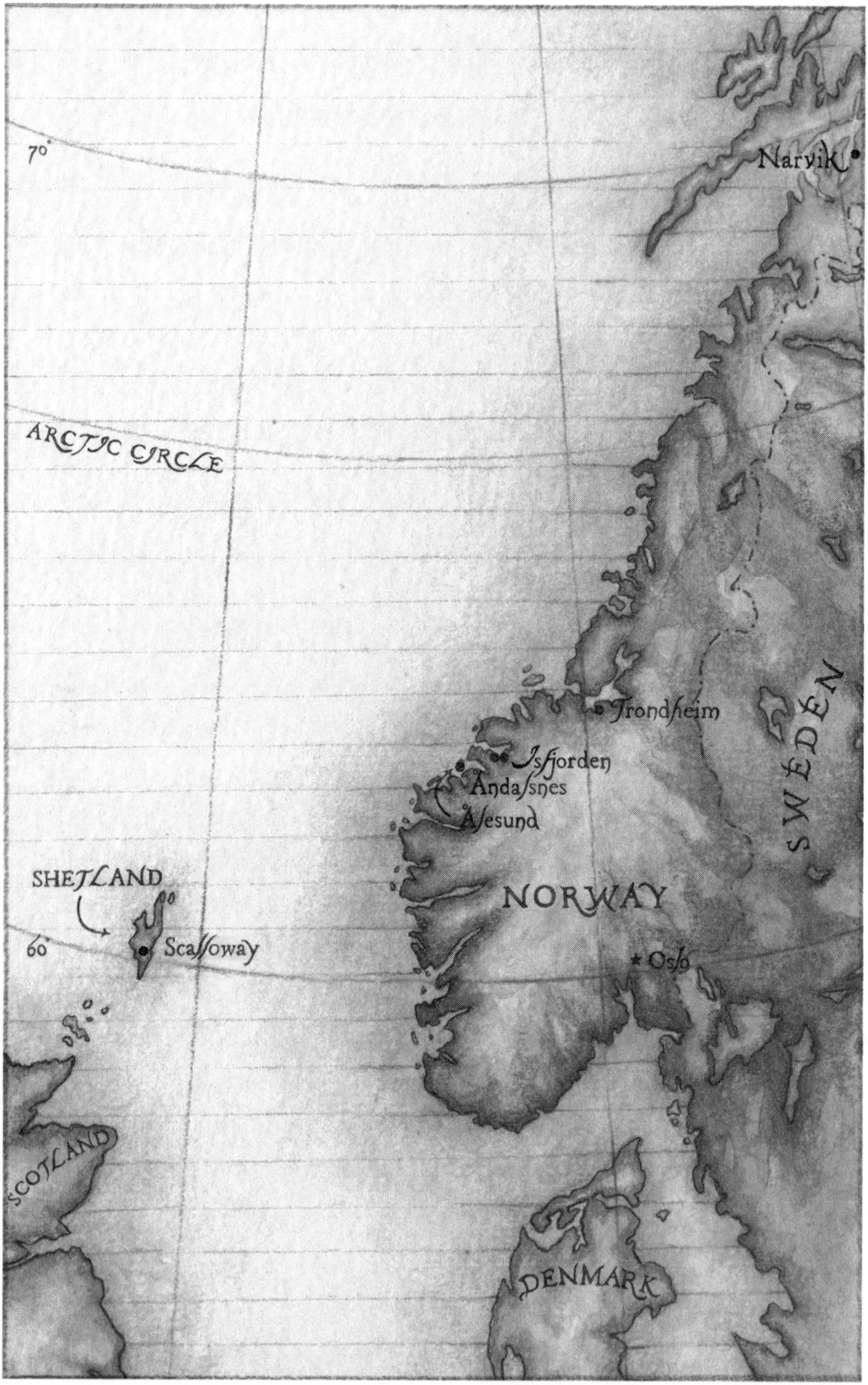

70°
Narvik
ARCTIC CIRCLE
Trondheim
Isfjorden
Andalsnes
Ålesund
SWEDEN
SHETLAND
NORWAY
60°
Scalloway
Oslo
SCOTLAND
DENMARK

# FOREWORD

*This story is based on events that followed the
sudden German invasion of Norway in the early morning
hours of April 9, 1940. Living under Nazi occupation,
countless ordinary Norwegian people—students, teachers,
pastors, fishermen—risked everything to keep
the hope of freedom alive.*

## CHAPTER ONE

# April 1940

In her dream, Marit raced Papa on her new wooden skis, farther and farther away from their *hytte*—their mountain cabin—and this time she was winning. Across the blinding whiteness, she pushed on, defying the mountains, said to be trolls turned to stone. She herringboned to the next peak, her thighs burning with the effort, then pushed off with her poles, and swooshed down through knee-deep powder.

An explosion wrenched Marit Gundersen from her sleep and shook her to her rib cage.

Wide-eyed, she bolted upright. Her skin prickled with fear. In near darkness, Marit flung back her feather-filled *dyne* and swung her legs over the bed's icy edge. What had startled her? Her mind darted back and forth. An early thunderstorm in the mountains? The train from Oslo—had it crashed? Had the steamer exploded in Romsdal Fjord?

Mama burst into Marit's room. "Marit!" she cried. "Get downstairs!"

"Mama, what's going on?" Surely there was an explanation and no need to panic.

But Mama's flannel nightgown swirled at her ankles as she turned to the hallway. "Come, Lars—you must wake up!"

Marit yanked a sweater over her nightgown, shoved her toes into her sheepskin slippers, and then stumbled from her room—right into Papa, his unlaced boots hitched over his pajama bottoms.

Marit squared her fists to her waist. "Papa, tell me what's going on—"

"Downstairs to the cellar!" he said, his hand firm on her shoulder as he guided her toward the stairs. "Questions later."

Mama dragged Lars through his bedroom doorway, but he pulled back against her hand and dropped in a heap on the floor.

"I don't want to," he moaned.

"Lars—wake up. I can't carry you!"

Shrill and piercing sounds whistled overhead, followed by a thunderous *boom-boom-boom!* Papa turned and scooped Lars over his shoulder—as if he had just turned three, not seven—and down the stairs they all flew.

The living room walls shuddered. Dishes rattled in the hutch, and the mantel clock and lamps crashed to the floor. Before Marit and her family had crossed the room, another explosion hit nearby—*boom!*—and the living room window shattered. Marit grabbed Papa's arm. "Papa, look." Beyond the empty frame, and under the questioning gaze of snow-topped mountains, strange planes wheeled through the dusky sky. The pounding continued.

"No time! Under the table!" Papa shouted.

They dived for shelter as an ear-ringing roar passed over them. Marit cowered. What in the world was happening? Though she was in grade four, old enough to brave many things—she was a fast skier, always the first of her friends to jump into the icy fjord waters in spring, the one who wanted to hike to the topmost peaks in the summer—now she barely knew herself. She clutched Mama's waist like a frightened toddler. With each explosion that shook the house, waves of fear rolled through her. Finally, a troubling quiet fell.

The house groaned with brokenness.

No one spoke until the last plane droned away.

Mama's blue eyes were set in an ash-darkened face, her normally blond hair now blackened with soot. "Marit, are you all right?"

How was she to answer? Nothing seemed real. Only yesterday they'd returned from skiing on their spring holiday. Only yesterday she'd left their grass-roofed *hytte* in the mountains. Only yesterday she'd laughed until her cheeks hurt. With a sunburned nose, she'd arrived home, ready to return to school. *Today.* She should be getting ready for school.

"Marit?" her mother repeated. "Can you hear me?"

Marit blinked dust from her eyes. "*Ja,* Mama. I'm all right."

Lars buried his face in the folds of Mama's nightgown and cried. "I'm scared!"

Her voice shaky, Mama comforted him. "We're fine," she said, smoothing his hair with the palm of her hand. "No one is hurt."

For several minutes they huddled beneath the table, as if the warmth of their bodies could protect them from what had happened. Marit pressed her head against Papa's chest. He wrapped his arm around her, his heart thudding against her ear. "We'll get through this," he said. Then he crawled out from their shelter and his boots crunched across glass to the broken window. He picked up his double-stringed fiddle from its fallen stand and shook out shards of glass. Holding it to his chest, he stared out the window. "Dear God—not Norway, too."

"Erik!" Mama said. "Get back—please."

He didn't move.

"But they might return any second."

"*Nei,* I think the Germans have done their damage . . . for the moment."

Marit's pulse thudded in her head and her stomach churned, but she finally found her voice. "Germans, Papa? Are you sure?"

"I'm sure. I saw the planes. Who else would invade us?"

"Invade," Marit ventured, "as in Austria and Poland?" Her parents had discussed the latest events throughout Europe every evening at the dinner table.

He was quiet for a long moment. "Marit, I don't know anything for sure yet. We need to find out who else was hit—what kind of damage has been done."

Limbs trembling, uncertain her legs would hold her, Marit crawled out from under the table. The hutch had hopped an arm's length from the corner, and Mama's teapot and porcelain plates lay in splinters. The pot-bellied cookstove tilted through the kitchen wall, leaving a gaping ragged hole.

Marit stepped closer and looked out. Dirt, boards, a bicycle wheel, and pieces of twisted metal littered the yard. Only yesterday four pairs of skis stood in fresh snow against the shed, but now they were scattered and broken matchsticks. More than once, her grandparents had boasted how Norway had avoided war for over a hundred years. They said Norway was a peaceful country that got along with its neighbors. This shouldn't be happening!

Village dogs began barking. Smoke rose above the trees and drifted in through the holes in her house's walls and windows. The wail of a woman came from somewhere beyond. Marit's hands fell to her sides and a vague numbness settled over her. Talk around the village had made her feel safe: "Norway stayed out of the Great War of 1914," someone had said. "We'll stay out of this one, too. Our king will see that we stay neutral." Everyone spoke with certainty that the Nazis would never invade Norway.

But now, it seemed, they had.

## CHAPTER TWO

# Leaving

Over the next few days, Marit refused to cry. Instead, she tried to be as helpful as possible—sweeping up glass, wiping down walls, scrubbing out cupboards, and restacking the woodpile. "Far better to stay busy," Mama said, "than to sit around worrying while we wait for news from friends and relatives."

When her best friend, Liv, who lived three houses away, had said she must go with her family to stay at a faraway farm, Marit asked, "But why? You can't leave. Can't you talk your parents into staying?"

"I'll show you why," Liv said, leading the way with a limp. After the bombing, the doctor had removed a splinter as big as a finger from her leg. It had flown through the air like an arrow and embedded itself in Liv's leg, leaving an angry red bruise behind. She picked a path through debris to where it looked like her dog had been digging a trench. "Here."

On hands and knees they peered beside the trench and looked under the foundation. A giant black bullet was wedged beneath the floor.

"It's a bomb," Liv said. "That's why we have to leave— just as soon as Mama's ready. Really, we shouldn't even be this close, but I wanted to show you—so you'd understand why I can't stay."

Marit cautiously eased away.

When it was time to say goodbye, the girls put their hands up and touched fingertips—a farewell they'd invented years earlier. "We'll see each other soon," Marit said, forcing a smile, though she doubted her own words. She didn't have an address to the farm where Liv was going. "It's a distant relative," Liv had explained. "My parents don't even know if he's alive. Haven't seen him in fifteen years—but we're going anyway." Once war started, how would Marit find her?

One day at dinner, Papa folded and refolded his hands, a certain sign he had something serious to say. "Marit and Lars," he began, "we contacted your aunt and grandfather and decided you'll be safer with them on the island."

Marit's forkful of potatoes stopped midway between

her plate and her mouth. She shouldn't be surprised. Everyone was talking of leaving, but leaving together—as families. "But we belong *here*—with you and Mama." Marit's voice rose. "You said, Papa, that 'we'll get through this,' remember? Why can't we stay together?"

Papa studied her, and for a moment, Marit thought he might agree. Then he said, "Cities and villages are targets for bombing. I know this is hard, but you two will be safer with Aunt Ingeborg and Bestefar. They'll take care of you, and, besides, you might learn something from them."

Through clamped teeth, Marit exhaled sharply. "But they're *not* you and Mama." She wanted to shout and cry all at once. How could she convince them? She couldn't be sent away. She needed to be with her parents. Didn't they understand? Only when she was with them did her fear begin to melt. Bestefar was as cold as fish scales! She'd never been able to do anything right around him, unlike her brother. "Then send Lars. Why can't I stay here?"

Mama reached for Marit's hands and held them in her own. "Your grandfather's not easy, I'll grant you that. But you'll be safe. That's our main concern. And you know Aunt Ingeborg adores you."

"I still don't get why *you* and Papa are staying here and sending *us* away." Marit squeezed back tears. "Why can't you come with us?"

Something in Papa's eyes told her there was no room for argument, that their decision was final. "Marit, right now," he said, "the less you know, the better."

That night, after Lars fell asleep, Papa motioned to Marit and Mama from his map-laden table. "I have news," he said. "And you must promise to keep this to yourselves."

Marit glanced at her father's maps. He always kept them neat and organized, but now many were ash-smudged and torn. She nodded, pleased to be invited in on his secret.

"Of course," Mama agreed.

"Boatloads of British soldiers have already landed in darkness at the end of our fjord. They've come because of Britain's own fight with Nazi Germany. They want to help Norway throw off the Germans."

Marit wondered why Papa was telling them all this. She glanced at Mama. The same question seemed to form in her eyes.

"We may have a British visitor sometime tonight. I don't want you to be scared."

"Who, Papa?"

"I don't know exactly."

"Will there be fighting here?"

Papa picked up his fiddle, rested it under his chin, and began to play a soft tune, as if to soothe her. "*Nei*, I hope not."

"What about your maps, Papa? Is the British visitor interested in your maps? Maybe that's why he's coming. If you need help with anything, you know I'd do whatever you and Mama asked, if only I can stay."

If she knew more, perhaps she could make sense of it all.

Later, a faint knock sounded downstairs at the back door. *Tap, tap. Tap, tap.*

Marit lay in bed, wide-eyed. Through her open door, she strained to hear.

"Come in," Papa said in a hushed voice. *"Velkommen."*

In broken Norwegian, a man greeted Papa and Mama, and then said, "Erik Gundersen, I'm told you know the mountains and roads better than anyone in this region."

Mama—who came from a family of teachers and taught English at the upper school—helped translate.

"What news have you heard of Oslo?" Papa asked. "Is the king safe?"

"King Haakon has fled. The Germans are eager to capture him, but so far he has eluded them."

The man went on to explain other events of the war, and Marit listened closely. He explained that the German attack was part of a full-scale invasion of Norway.

"I can understand their targeting Oslo and the larger cities, but Isfjorden?" Papa asked. "We're a village. It makes no sense."

Mama interpreted the soldier's reply. "You're at the

end of the fjord, right across from the Åndalnes port and train depot. That puts this region at risk. The Germans —they want to shatter Norway with one sudden and decisive blow."

"But we're Norwegians," Papa said, anger nearly crushing his voice. A moment of silence passed before he spoke again. "We won't fall that easily."

The man lowered his voice. "We hope not, and that's why we need to work together. I understand you might both be helpful. We need engineers who know the area and we need good translators, too."

Then the door to the staircase was closed, and their voices blurred.

But Marit had heard enough. She was right. Papa's knowledge of the terrain and his engineering skills were going to be used to fight the Germans. And if they needed translators, who could do a better job than Mama, who already taught English? Perhaps her parents would come to realize that they might need extra help. She could do whatever they needed—run errands, deliver messages, help around the home.

Marit was determined to stay awake until the man left, and then ask her parents about his visit. There must be something she could do to help.

But she never got the chance. When she awoke, everything happened with the speed of startled birds. Before she knew it, she was packing her suitcase, picking her path through her yard, and walking down the bomb-damaged streets to the harbor.

Together with her family, she passed neighbors still at work repairing homes and shops. Some homes were shattered beyond fixing. Before, she would have felt too old to hold Mama's hand in public; now she held on tightly. Everything had changed. It was as if she was watching a girl her age from a great distance—the blond braid that touched her waist, the red and white snowflake sweater, hiking boots and rucksack ... the little brother in his blue wool jacket and the parents. ... But nothing about them seemed real. This couldn't possibly be *her* family heading to the dock to wait for the steamer that would ferry her and Lars down Romsdal Fjord—away from home.

As they waited, Mama handed Marit a small basket filled with smoked salmon, cheese, bread, and a jar of milk. But Marit doubted she could eat anything. Her throat tightened with tears.

At the end of the fjord and protected by mountains, her village had always felt safe. Now, scraps of wooden boats filled the harbor and their charred masts poked up like old bones. Stone chimneys stood tall amid piles of burned boards. Wisps of smoke climbed from the rubble. How dare the Nazis invade them? She wanted to scream at the Germans who had dropped the bombs. Didn't they have families, too?

The steamer chugged around the fjord's bend, and Papa knelt and hugged her and Lars close. "Bestefar will meet you two in Ålesund—and then he'll ferry you with his boat back to the island." He paused, as if searching for something more to say. Finally, he stood and said only, "I promise—we'll be together soon."

"Then please," Marit burst out, "please—don't send us away!" She wrapped her arms around her mother. Her entire life was being ripped up by the roots.

Too soon, with Lars at her heels, Marit boarded the steamer. As the engine rumbled and the steamer pulled away and out of the harbor, she raced up the ladder to the stern railing. She had meant to wave goodbye; instead, she gripped the wooden rail and looked back through blurry eyes. Something larger and more frightening than she could possibly understand had been set in motion. Beyond the steamer's churning wake, Mama and Papa became smaller and smaller, until she could not see them at all.

Hours later, the steamer eased toward the landing. Fog thick as *risengrøt*—Marit's favorite rice pudding—covered the city's harbor as the steamer slowed its engine. Marit kept a lookout for Bestefar's boat, which was like many other fishing trawlers with its two masts, open decks, wheelhouse, and the *tonk-tonk-tonk* of its engine. They were sturdy wooden boats that handled wind or calm, port or open ocean water.

In the fog, everything was gray and dull. On past holidays, she had loved looking at Ålesund's ornate and colorful buildings. She loved walking past the bustling wharves and fisheries where they turned dry, salted cod into klipfish and shipped it around the world. Once dried and salted, the codfish kept forever. She loved Mama's way of cooking it in butter and water. Though the fisheries used faster, more modern methods, some local fishermen still dried split cod on large boulders in the sun.

She spotted the trawler dockside. Two masts stood tall, the wheelhouse was empty, and Bestefar sat on the rail, his legs crossed in wool trousers, cupping a pipe. "There he is, Lars."

"Bestefar!" Lars called as he ran ahead down the steamer's rough planks, but their grandfather didn't hear. His head was bowed.

Marit followed behind, making her way slowly toward the fishing trawler.

Bestefar looked up and saw them coming. He held up his hand, probably the friendliest gesture Marit guessed she would see from him.

"*Hei*, Bestefar," Marit called, trying to force a little cheerfulness in her voice.

He nodded at them. "Hurry now." Beneath his fisherman's wool cap, tufts of white hair stuck out, matching his well-trimmed mustache. His steely eyes seemed harder than ever. Mama always said he was a happier man when Bestemor—Marit's grandmother—was alive. But she'd died when Marit was only three, too young to remember her. "It's as if your grandmother's long illness drained the life out of him, too," Mama had once tried to explain. "Not only did Ingeborg take over Mama's classroom on the island, but she stayed on at home to care for Papa. He wouldn't leave the house for days, not eating, not even tending his nets. It was your aunt Ingeborg who finally forced him from the house and back to fishing again."

Marit wished she could feel sorry for him, but the only grandfather she'd ever known was cold and short on words—except with Lars, of course.

"Lars," Bestefar said. "You're getting to be a big man now."

Lars jumped right into Bestefar's arms. "Not that big, Bestefar!"

Marit turned away. He hadn't even said hello to her or used her name. If he wanted to be that way, she could too. Let him be in his own salty broth, like herring in a barrel.

"Well, don't just stand there on the dock, Marit. Cast

off now. And no falling in this time. I don't want to fish you out again."

"Bestefar, that was a long time ago." She'd been four when she'd tripped and gone in, nearly drowning. Why couldn't he let it go? Swiftly, she moved to untie the line from the nearest cleat. In her haste, however, she managed to make knots in the rope where there had been none. She felt Bestefar's eyes on her, waiting. She was making a mess of things only because of him. It was the way he was. Nothing was ever done quite right. Never fast enough.

With the rope finally untied, Marit pushed off from the dock and jumped into the boat. The sails were down and secured. Her grandfather ran the engine for the short trip back to the island. He stood in the wheelhouse. Lars stood in front of him, a big smile on his face, hands up on the wheel, pretending to steer beneath Bestefar's large hands.

Seagulls swooped and cried mournfully around the boat as it crossed from the mainland to Godøy Island. Marit stood at the bow and clung to the rails. Salt water splashed up as the bow rose and fell. She breathed in the salty ocean air. She hated to leave her parents, but at least the island was a place she loved to visit. She loved combing the shoreline for treasures. There were the chickens and goats, and Big Olga, with her gentle brown eyes, the cow Marit had learned to milk years earlier. And Aunt Ingeborg. She was like a crab, hard-shelled on the outside, but soft on the inside. Strict, too, but she had to be. She was a schoolteacher.

Compared with her aunt, Bestefar was . . . Marit glanced back at the snow-crowned mountains. She had it. He was a stone troll.

### CHAPTER THREE

# Land of the Midnight Sun

On summer nights, the sun held fast to the sky, refusing to let darkness swallow the land. Whenever Marit opened her eyes, a hazy light covered the island and poured in through the open window. And this night was no different. She drifted on a sea of frustration, a rowboat tossed by every wave.

The bed she shared with Lars barely fit in the room. It may have been her mother's room when she was a girl, but it was never meant to be shared by two—especially with a younger brother. If Lars slept soundly, then he didn't wet their shared bed. If he slept fitfully and cried out from nightmares, then Marit hung sheets on the clothesline the next morning. Marit envied Aunt Ingeborg sleeping in a bed all by herself in the other upstairs bedroom.

She felt trapped, pushed up against the wall, but at least on her side of the bed, a window looked out toward the sea.

The pasture ended at the shore and rocky peninsula, and at the base of the lighthouse paced a German soldier, his rifle angled on his shoulder. Immediately after the first bombs fell, truckloads of German soldiers arrived and took control of every town in Norway. At first, they handed out candy, which she always refused. Every time Marit saw them, an icy unease settled in her belly. The Nazi soldiers patrolled everywhere, including the islands. And this soldier, guarding this lighthouse, came too close. As far back as she could remember, she'd loved walking out to the lighthouse. It was as much her own as it was every Norwegian's lighthouse.

Over two months had passed since the Germans had dropped bombs and invaded. It was already June. Though more bombs fell up and down Norway's coast, none had yet fallen on Godøy Island. And in all that time—since the day she and Lars had arrived at the island—she hadn't heard from Mama and Papa. *Not a word.* They were her parents. Why didn't they write? Or leave a message on the phone at the island's general store? Phone lines might be down, her parents were likely helping the British, but things still didn't add up. The British and Norwegians had failed to stop the Germans. The Nazis were rumored to make many unexpected arrests, and when they did, people disappeared. What if Mama and Papa were arrested in Isfjorden? What if she never heard from them again?

With a small kick, Marit untangled her legs from her nightdress. She checked on Lars, to see if he was twitching with nightmares. He slept stomach-down, burrowed in his pillow, his hair rumpled around his head. He breathed slowly, peacefully; otherwise—just to be safe— Marit would have nudged him to get up and use the night pot.

She flopped back down, shifting from her belly to her back. Day by day, there were more orphans in Norway. At least she wasn't one of them. She dropped her forearm across her eyes. But nothing worked.

Finally, Marit gave up and studied the buttery yellow slanted ceiling, the hand-painted chest that held her traveling clothes, and above it on the windowsill, the jar of daisies Lars had gathered alongside the dirt road. She rolled over, facing the wall. Papa had promised they'd be together soon. But when was "soon"? Two months, two years? *When, Papa?* They should never have left Isfjorden—no matter how bad things had seemed; they should have stayed together as a family.

Marit curled into a tight ball and finally slept.

*"Frokost!"* Aunt Ingeborg called upstairs, as she did every morning. Marit jumped up, emerging from a dream of searching for her parents amid bomb-shelled buildings, and bumped her head on the slanted ceiling. *"Uff da!"*

With a groan, she dragged herself out of bed. The sun was higher than usual. "Oh, no." By now, Big Olga's udder would be painfully full.

Lars's rumpled hair—the color of *kaffe* with cream—stuck out from under the fluffy *dyne*.

"Lars, get up. Don't keep Aunt Ingeborg waiting."

No sooner had the words left her tongue than the *dyne* flew off the bed. As Lars's feet hit the wooden floor, Marit hurried ahead down the steep stairs into the yeast-scented kitchen. She braced herself for her aunt's scolding, although the worst kind of scolding was Bestefar's stony silence.

Aunt Ingeborg turned away from her bread dough and wiped her flour-dusted hands on her apron. Her fingernails were trimmed short, her forearms covered with sun-bleached hairs and sprinkled with freckles from hours in the gardens. She pushed golden strands back into her tightly woven bun, then humphed.

"I thought you were going to sleep forever. The sun's halfway through its chores already, as you two should be." She had the same sterling blue eyes as Mama—only

Mama's eyes were glistening water, and Aunt Ingeborg's were melting ice.

At the back door, Marit pulled on her boots. "I'm sorry . . ." she began. "I'm going right now."

"No, I already took care of the milking. Boots off." Aunt Ingeborg patted Marit's shoulder and steered her to a chair at the table. It was set with plates of cheese, herring, bread, strawberry jam, and hard-boiled eggs and a pitcher of buttermilk. "Besides, you needed extra sleep. A girl of ten shouldn't have such dark circles."

"*Takk.* Tomorrow—I promise—I'll be up earlier."

"Tomorrow, *ja,* but today I need you two to pick rhubarb."

"For pie?" Lars asked, his dimples deepening in his rounded cheeks.

"And jam. I hope to trade some for flour and a little coffee. Now, bow your heads."

Later, they headed outside. Alongside the red barn, trimmed white like every door and window frame of her grandfather's goldenrod house, they found rhubarb leaves as big as elephant's ears. In the land of the midnight sun, the long hours of daylight helped crops grow fast—and large.

"Remember, Lars," Marit said, "pull them out like this." Without breaking its stem, she pulled on a long rhubarb stalk until it slipped free.

"I *know,* Marit," Lars said, shaking his head. "I heard

what Aunt Ingeborg said. You don't always have to tell me what to do, just because you're older." His bangs hung nearly into his eyes; Mama would have trimmed his hair weeks ago.

Marit put her hand on his shoulder. "I know you're smart. You finished grade one already."

Lars lowered his head.

"Well, maybe you didn't *finish* grade one, but close enough."

"See?" he said. "You said I didn't finish."

"Don't worry—we'll start school in the fall and you'll be in grade two."

He was two heads shorter, but sturdy. The island was a good place for him, and Aunt Ingeborg's cooking had helped ease the stomachaches he'd had when they first arrived.

Some things were the same. Her brother. Aunt Ingeborg and Bestefar. Three cows swishing their tails in the pasture. The island smells of kelp, fish, and salt water. Cries of seagulls and kittiwakes. Wooden trawlers and smaller fishing boats bobbing on a soft chop. The fairyland city of Ålesund across the harbor with its towers and turrets—or at least what was left of it. But when sirens rang across the water, the sound of bombs falling in Ålesund often followed.

She turned away and joined Lars in picking more rhubarb. Soon a pile of green leaves and red stalks reached Marit's knees. They brought their harvest to the back steps, cut off the stems, and threw the leaves behind the barn.

"Just enough sugar left to bake pies," Aunt Ingeborg said as they carried the ruby red stems into her tidy kitchen. "After this, I don't know when we'll see sugar again."

## CHAPTER FOUR

# Refugee

That afternoon—as they had every Monday, Wednesday, and Saturday since they'd arrived—Marit and Lars hiked the dirt road to the fishing wharf. They paused by the first boathouse, where a new propaganda poster had been tacked up overnight. The illustration showed a blond Norwegian and a blond German shaking hands, with *"Alt for Norge!"* written above it.

"Don't believe it," she told Lars. *"All for Norway* is a lie."

Such posters often combined Nazi swastikas with Viking boats and heroic characters, as if the Germans could convince Norwegians that the two countries were destined to merge. Norwegians regularly ripped down the pro-Nazi posters at night, but in the mornings, German soldiers tacked them back up again.

Beneath the gaze of Godøy Mountain, Marit and Lars walked on. They passed several island farms—narrow strips of land that stretched like piano keys to the shore. Fjord horses dotted a few pastures; more ponies than horses, their thick manes and golden coats caught the morning sunlight as they grazed.

Along the way, Marit's mind raced with worry that a letter from Mama and Papa might—or might not—arrive. At least there was one bright spot: her new friend, Hanna.

The day they'd first met, Marit had been waiting on the pier with other islanders for the mail boat to arrive. Someone had tapped Marit on her shoulder and asked, "Where are *you* from?" Marit turned to discover a girl her own height, with shiny dark hair and a smile that revealed a slice of air between her front teeth.

"Isfjorden," Marit replied.

"My name's Hanna Brottem. What's yours?"

"Marit Gundersen. I'm staying with my grandfather, Leif Halversen, and my aunt Ingeborg."

"You mean Miss Halversen. She's going to be my teacher next fall."

"Really? Oh, and this is my brother, Lars."

Lars glanced away shyly, but his dimples deepened. *"Hei,"* he said, without meeting Hanna's eyes.

Hanna told Marit about her family's new baby and two-year-old sister she looked after every day while her mother worked at the hospital in Ålesund. She pointed to a nearby red clapboard home facing the ocean. And Marit told Hanna about being bombed, how their cookstove had been blown partway through their kitchen wall, and how they hadn't been able to return home yet. That she wondered every day if her parents were all right.

"That's terrible," Hanna said. "Much worse than no flour or sugar."

"A lot worse."

Hanna's eyebrows bunched over her tiny nose. "Then . . . you're *refugees*."

*Refugees*. The word had an edge to it, like a fence meant to divide those who belong from those who do not. Marit wasn't sure if this girl was making fun of her. What had she meant exactly? She bristled. *"Ja*. I guess so."

Hanna touched her arm lightly. "That must be hard— to be separated like that from your home and parents."

Marit could only nod. Whatever doubts Marit had about Hanna instantly vanished. She knew she'd made a good friend.

As they waited for the mail boat to pull alongside the dock, Marit tapped her foot impatiently. Lars held

Marit's hand, and she let him. His small hand reminded her that he was only seven. Even at ten, she was having a terrible time being separated from Mama and Papa. More than once, she'd woken up from the same nightmare. Always, she was on a ship with her family and they were crossing the ocean, when out of nowhere, the legendary sea monster—the *kraken*—reached its terrible tentacles and suction cups around the ship and to the very top of the mast. Part crab, part octopus, it was enormous, and it finally found what it was looking for—Mama and Papa. It wrapped its slimy arms around their bodies and pulled them toward its pinching mouth, then sank out of sight, leaving a whirlpool behind. Marit clung to Lars as the ship twirled in dizzying circles, sucked slowly downward toward the bottom of the sea. That's when she usually woke up—terrified and sobbing.

"*Hei,* Marit!" Hanna ran toward them, her braids whipping in the breeze. Marit dropped Lars's hand. "Hanna!"

Soon after, the mail boat pulled up to the main dock.

"What do you have for us today?" called Mr. Larsen, grabbing a line and tying it off. Owner of the general store, with a head of short sandy curls and matching beard, he was taller than most men on the island.

"The usual," replied the captain. He tossed the leather mailbag to Mr. Larsen as a handful of passengers disembarked.

"Do you have a letter from the Gundersens?" Marit asked Mr. Larsen, following him step by step to his shop.

"Same answer, Marit. You'll have to wait—along with everyone else."

A new sign in the window stated: *Out of potatoes. Don't know when we'll get them.*

Inside, the shop's shelves of food, household, and farm supplies seemed to dwindle every day. Mr. Larsen stood behind his counter and began pulling letters and parcels from the leather bag. Villagers crowded around. "Ivarsen!" he called out.

"Here!" A young woman scurried forward, hand up.

"Riste."

"Over here." Marit recognized the fisherman who held his pipe in the air. He was a friend of Bestefar's.

With each name that Mr. Larsen called, Marit's dread grew that they would *never* get a letter, *never* again see Mama and Papa. To again hear nothing, to walk back along the road empty-handed, to be passed by truckloads of German soldiers . . . A stone lodged in her throat and she chewed the inside of her lip to keep from crying. If she started, she'd never stop.

Hanna elbowed her. "Marit—he called Halversen. Raise your hand."

Marit shot her hand up and hurried forward. She suddenly couldn't speak.

Mr. Larsen looked over her head, waving the letter high. "Halversen?"

"Here!" She waved her arm back and forth.

Suddenly, the chatter in the shop died away as Mr. Larsen turned toward the window, the letter frozen in his hand. Everyone followed his gaze. Outside, a German officer dismounted from his bay horse, its coat as glossy as its rider's long black boots. When the Germans had arrived, they'd brought their own horses with them.

The officer stepped inside and frowned, as if he'd caught a group of children doing something wrong. "Too many," he said in halting Norwegian, his nose bent slightly at the bridge. He waved his arm through the air as if clearing unwelcome cobwebs. "A secret meeting?"

Mr. Larsen spoke up, waving the letter. "I was just handing out the mail. You see? This one goes to the Halversens." He pointed to Marit. "Marit and her brother are grandchildren of Leif Halversen."

The German studied Marit.

She held herself back from leaping for the letter like a starving dog after a food scrap. She kept calm—controlling herself—as if the letter meant nothing to her at all. But she had already noticed the handwriting. It was Mama's!

The officer took the letter from Mr. Larsen's hand and placed it in Marit's. "There you go, *Fräulein*."

She would rather spit in his hand than take anything from him, but she couldn't refuse the letter. It burned between her fingers. She wanted to rip it open, but instead she waited for the officer to leave. As soon as he was outside and turned his tall, ebony horse toward the street, Marit hurried to the door, with Hanna and Lars right behind her.

Once outside, she studied the letter.

"Is it from your parents?" Hanna asked.

"*Nei.* I mean, the return address says Siversen, not Gundersen. But the handwriting. Something's not right. I'm sure this is my mother's."

"Hanna! Marit!" came a familiar voice. The girls looked up from the envelope. Olaf, a year older and a friend of Hanna's, hurried from the docks toward them, all smiles. In his arms he carried a shaggy pup. The dog's eyes were mismatched—one was blue, the other brown—and its pink tongue lapped relentlessly at Olaf's face. "Look what my father brought back for me from Ålesund! It's a husky—the kind that pulls sleds."

He set the wiggly puppy down on the side of the road and combed the pup's thick fur with his fingers. The puppy's tail curved over its back. "He's going to be a fine dog, don't you think? And big. Just look at his paws."

The puppy was cute, but Marit could only think of the letter and getting home so she could read it with Aunt Ingeborg. "C'mon, Lars. We have to go."

But Lars dropped to his knees and hugged the puppy's neck. He was always quick to fall in love with animals. "*Hei*, little puppy—"

"What are you going to name him?" Hanna asked, squatting down alongside Lars.

Olaf's eyes flickered with mischief. "I was thinking of calling him Marit."

"*Nei!*" Marit tried to pretend outrage, but she knew Olaf was teasing.

"Actually, I'm thinking of calling him Kaptain."

"I like that," Hanna said.

At that moment, nothing besides the letter mattered. "Lars," she said, "we need to get back." She sounded as firm as Aunt Ingeborg and pulled him to his feet. "I'm sure we'll see Kaptain again soon. We have chores."

"Marit . . . but—"

"Now!" She nearly ran all the way home, but had to keep stopping along the road to wait for Lars to catch up. Past the school building, boathouses, and pastures, they followed the road as it curved northeast. As they turned down the dirt drive and raced past the barn, the goats lifted their heads in question.

Aunt Ingeborg met Marit on the doorstep. "Marit— what is it? What's the matter?"

Out of breath, Marit handed her the letter and stepped in. Aunt Ingeborg sat down at the kitchen table and stared at the letter in her hands.

"It's Mama's writing, isn't it?" Marit said.

Aunt Ingeborg nodded. "Sure looks like it, but . . ."

For what seemed like a decade, Aunt Ingeborg held the letter, and then she set it on the woven table runner. "We'll read it when Bestefar returns."

"But—" Marit started to protest.

"Bestefar will be home soon." Aunt Ingeborg set her jaw, as she often did when asked questions that were too personal or important.

"But I can't wait!" Marit said.

"You have to." And with that, Marit knew the discussion was over.

The cookstove and counter boasted jars and jars of rhubarb-strawberry jam and four pies with lightly browned edges, which Marit had shaped with her thumb and forefingers before they'd left to meet the mail boat. Aunt Ingeborg hung up her apron.

"*Tusen takk,* you two. Your mother would be proud of you for all your help today. Let's put all this away to keep busy until Bestefar comes home."

Finally, the door rattled and Bestefar stepped in, his face etched from the wind and sun. Before Marit could reach for the letter, Aunt Ingeborg grabbed it from the table. "It looks like Kirsten's writing."

Bestefar studied the print, and they followed him as he settled on the back steps. He read the letter aloud.

It was from his "old friend Mrs. Siversen," whose house had been bombed and who was working with her husband in the mountains.

> *We're keeping in touch with our new friends and working hard these days. We think of you always and hope you understand our need to work toward the best country possible for our children.*

"It's like a message in code," Marit said. "It's Mama, for sure, and Papa, but they don't want to use their real names. And the British—those must be the 'new friends.' The mountains must mean up at the *hytte,* or somewhere away from Isfjorden. And the children—that's me and Lars."

As Bestefar sat reading, Aunt Ingeborg stood aside; they maintained their usual distance from each other. "Marit and Lars," Bestefar said, "you must not say a word about this letter to anyone."

"But why? I don't understand why—"

"Marit." Bestefar's brows hooded his eyes like an owl's. "It's dangerous. The Nazis are opening mail before it reaches its rightful owner. If anyone involved in Resistance activities is caught . . . well, I don't expect you to understand."

She crossed her arms against her chest—and against

him. He treated her worse than he treated his farm animals. At least he talked to them. She was a smart, hardworking student, yet he spoke to her only when he had to, as if she didn't have a brain in her head.

A gray goat wandered over to the back steps. Lars grabbed a curved horn and scratched the tuft of fur beneath the goat's chin. "The letter means they're all right," he said.

This time, her little brother had been quicker to grasp the heart of things.

"That's right, Lars," Bestefar said.

Aunt Ingeborg smiled faintly, clasped her hands beneath her chin, and whispered, "Thank God they're alive."

CHAPTER FIVE

# Turmoil on the Sea

The next morning, after milking, Marit let Big Olga out to pasture. As soon as Lars finished scattering feed for the chickens, they joined Aunt Ingeborg and Bestefar for coffee and a heart-shaped *vaffel* with a dab of jam. Marit loved coffee with lots and lots of cream and sugar, but now with shortages, she stirred only a spoonful of milk in hot water instead.

They couldn't afford to waste a crumb or drop of anything. In cities, even eggs and milk were hard to come by. At least on the farm, they could produce much of their own food.

The familiar rumble of a wood-fired German truck

engine rolled into the farmyard. Marit hated these visits the Germans made to collect their "daily donation."

Bestefar snorted, cup in hand. "*Ja*—produce for the Germans. They get fed first from Norway's food supply. We get the crumbs." Bestefar pushed back his chair. "Stay inside."

Marit jumped from her chair to the window. From the back of the canvas-topped truck, a soldier, not much older than a schoolboy, hopped out. He straightened his *jakke* and touched the gun in his holster. He spoke a word or two to Bestefar, who disappeared into the barn and returned with two baskets of produce.

Like a fog suddenly lifting, Marit's sense of caution evaporated. She bolted toward the door, turned the handle, and bravely stepped out.

"Marit," Aunt Ingeborg scolded, "what are you doing?"

But Marit was already closing the door behind her and walking straight toward Bestefar, who held out a basket full of strawberries and lettuce to the soldier. He tossed her a warning glance. The soldier waited as Bestefar went back into the barn.

Marit's feet became rocks. She was standing alone with the soldier, something she hadn't intended. Through his wire rims, he studied her. "Have you a name, *Fräulein*?"

She stared at the ground.

"You needn't be afraid," he said. "We're not monsters."

*Nei,* she screamed inside, *you're worse than monsters!*

Seconds seemed to expand into hours, and to her relief, Bestefar returned, this time lugging a basket of brown eggs and a milk can.

"Is that all?" the young soldier demanded, as if he were suddenly ruler and king. How dare he come and demand food, then act as if their hard-gathered donations weren't enough! She glared at the soldier.

"I'm a fisherman-farmer," Bestefar said evenly. "We have only a few chickens, goats, and cows—and only one milking cow."

"We ask the animals to speed up their production," Marit added with an exaggerated shrug, "but they just continue at their same slow pace." Then she shook her head side to side and kept a straight face, just the way Papa would after making a joke. Inside, she felt boldly triumphant.

Bestefar froze. Only his fingertips twitched at his sides.

The soldier glared at her, then turned on his heels and strode to his supply truck with the goods. He returned with empty baskets and an empty milk can to be filled again on his next visit. Then he jumped in the truck, rapped his knuckles on the door panel, and the vehicle rumbled on to the next fisherman's farm.

Marit waited, her shoulders tensed toward her ears.

"Marit!" Bestefar's voice carried the sting of a wasp. He pointed toward the empty road. "What in God's good heaven were you thinking? You could have been arrested and hauled away. Never, *ever* do that again! I told you to stay inside. You're not to speak a word to them. Such joking could get you—and all of us—in trouble."

Bombs had fallen on her village. The smell of smoke over Isfjorden had lingered for days. She had been separated for so long from Mama and Papa. The Germans were the cause of all of it. Yet Bestefar gave the Nazis everything they asked for. He almost made it *easy* for them.

"Walk with me," Bestefar ordered and headed into the pasture. Marit followed reluctantly, picking her path carefully between the cowpies. Grazing along the distant fence, Big Olga lifted her head and stared at them, chewing her cud. Finally, Bestefar stopped beside a large boulder that jutted out of the middle of the field. "Sit down."

She sat cross-legged on the sun-warmed, ancient boulder, her feet dangling. Bestefar clasped his hands behind his back. Marit followed his gaze. The field sloped and ended in a peninsula; from there, the breakwater extended to the lighthouse.

"In Oslo," he said, his voice low and matter-of-fact, "some young men bombed a bridge between the city and the airport. They thought they were hurting the Germans, but what did the Germans do? They posted threats. Anyone connected with the destruction of the bridge would be executed. Not only that, they warned that the local people would suffer as well." He paused. "It makes no sense to have a whole town suffer for the acts of a few." He turned and looked at her. "Do you see how complicated it gets?"

She couldn't believe he was actually speaking to her. She didn't know if he wanted an answer or not, but she gathered her courage. "But Bestefar, if no one fights back, the Germans will be here *forever!*"

"Perhaps it's better to keep the peace, no matter what, and not put family and friends in danger. We're a peace-loving, neutral country. We've stayed out of wars for many years and we need to stay out of this one, too."

She'd heard that kind of thinking before.

"No good can come of getting involved," he went on. "The Germans will respect our neutrality, you'll see. They're at war with the Allied countries, not with us. They want access to our coastlines, nothing more."

She didn't believe that for a second. Memories of whistling bombs pressed in on her, and she clasped her arms around her waist. Maybe Bestefar was living in a dream. *His* island, *his* home, hadn't been bombed. "And what about Mama and Papa?" she said. "They would rather be with us here, but they're staying in Isfjorden to help the British fight against the Nazis. Should they 'stay out'?"

Bestefar returned his gaze toward the lighthouse where the soldiers kept a constant guard. "Your father has always been a dreamer, Marit. An idealist. He's putting his life and your mother's in danger. It's folly, pure and simple. He's a fool."

Papa a fool? Nothing could be further from the truth. How could Bestefar say such things? *"Nei!"* she said, speaking to his back. "He's brave and so is Mama. At least they're doing *something!*"

Bestefar was silent; his fisherman's sweater rose and fell with his breaths as he looked off to sea.

Without a word or his permission to leave, Marit jumped off the boulder and ran back across the pasture, her throat on fire with all the things she wished she could say.

## CHAPTER SIX

# The Lighthouse

Boathouses lined the harbor, their slate roofs matching the grayish blue sea. At the last boathouse, Bestefar was bent over nets and glass floats on the dock. After their morning argument, Marit didn't care to talk with him again, but Lars had asked if they could take out the rowboat. And rowing would help clear her mind.

The pea-pod-shaped rowboat was pulled up on shore. Marit ran her hand along the weathered gunwale. The blue seats were in need of painting soon. The ribs of the boat needed a coat of varnish. Still, the memory of rowing with her mother gave her a sharp pang. Mama had taught her to row when Marit was only five years old. They'd pretended they were floating on the water in the belly of a whale, and that she and her mother were, like Jonah from the Bible story, ready to be spat out onto the sands of a new land. And that's exactly how Marit now felt on this isolated island.

She inhaled the sea-scented air. She wanted to take out the boat—to get away, if only a short distance. But would Bestefar let her? Mama had once explained that long before Marit was born they'd lost Karsten—her mother's and aunt's younger brother—when he was swimming and pulled out by a tide. "Since then," Mama had explained, "Bestefar's been worried about children and water. First he lost Karsten and later your grandmother took ill. Sometimes life is too hard."

"Bestefar, may we take out the rowboat?" she called as sweetly as she could muster.

He lifted his head and didn't answer.

"I used to row with Mama, remember?"

Bestefar dropped his net and crossed his arms. His eyebrows gathered in watchfulness. He opened his mouth.

Before he could say no, she added, "We'll stay close to the shore and not go far. Promise."

He shook his head. "I'm afraid not. There are explosives—floating mines—in the channels."

Marit stood still, her hand stopped on the boat's bow.

"Bestefar," Lars called in his singsong voice. "Please? We'll stay close. We won't go far."

Marit glanced at Bestefar. *Unbelievable!* Lars's dimply

smile softened up Bestefar's stern face every time. That Lars was his favorite was more than obvious.

Bestefar looked to the water, as if considering the sun glinting off the softly rippled surface. "Well, it's a calm day, and if you stay close to shore, between here and the lighthouse, where I can see you . . . within sight! Marit, you're in charge."

Favorite or not, she smiled. Soon, she was straining her muscles against the oars as their rowboat furrowed through water.

From the stern seat, Lars faced Marit. With her back to the bow, she rowed, glancing occasionally over her shoulder to make sure she was staying on the course she intended. It would be easier if she could face forward and see where she was going, but rowboats didn't work best that way.

"Marit, look!" Lars pointed over the edge of the rowboat. "A jellyfish! A bluish green one."

"Don't touch it."

"I know, you don't have to tell me."

Jellyfish always reminded her of pulsing raw yolks, and Marit did her best to avoid them if they floated up onshore. She didn't want to get stung.

She leaned forward, oar handles meeting close, then pulled back hard, elbows out, back muscles flexing. Shimmery jewels dropped from the tips of the oars as they swept across the water. Over and over, Marit sliced into the ocean current, losing herself in the rhythm and occasionally glancing over her shoulder toward the lighthouse. For the first time in months she felt a little like her old self: without a care and ready for adventure. She strained against the oars while Lars faced her from the stern, smiling and humming.

She rowed past farms and toward the lighthouse and peninsula that marked the tip of their pastureland. When she used to row with Mama, they'd stop near the lighthouse at the cove to explore what the tide had left behind. Easing up on the oars, Marit let the boat glide forward onto the gravel shore. She hopped out and pulled the boat up higher on the beach; Lars stumbled out after her.

At the end of the breakwater, three soldiers manned the base of the lighthouse. Marit grabbed Lars's hand, trying to pretend this was like all the other summers— the summers before swarms of gray-green uniforms had descended on the island. With guns angled over their shoulders, the soldiers watched them.

"Remember the time we found that old chain?" she asked Lars.

"From the Vikings, right Marit?"

"Of course!" It was kinder to go along with his imagination. She doubted the chain they'd found was that old.

She knew the soldiers were watching them. She felt

their cold, constant presence—their eyes on every movement. In past summers, when her family had visited, she and Lars always ran straight to the shoreline and combed it for treasures. Once she found a small blue bottle. When she poured out the seawater, a tiny crab slipped out of its shelter. The bottle sat on her bedroom shelf along with seashells she'd collected over the years. She hoped it would all still be there when she returned home.

Lars trailed her as she walked along the shoreline. At the water's edge, a slick black film covered several pieces of lumber and sticks. The smell was pungent, not the natural odor of kelp, but of bombs and fuel.

"Marit, what's that slimy stuff?"

"Hitler's hair tonic."

"What's that?"

Some jokes were lost on little kids. "Oh, skip it. There must have been an oil leak from a ship recently bombed at sea."

A few meters away, a small mound moved amid the seaweed.

"What's that?" Lars asked.

She picked her way closer. "Let's have a look."

Lars hung back. "Marit, maybe it's something poisonous."

A month earlier, when she'd walked from the pasture to the shore, she'd found two dead birds—a puffin and a cormorant. The same black deadly slime had coated their wings. She'd asked Bestefar and he'd said there was nothing they could do. He also explained that the Germans expected the Allied forces to invade along the coast, so they bombed any ship or fishing boat that looked suspicious, leaving fuel on the water. The Germans were shipping iron ore from Narvik in the north to keep their war across Europe supplied with steel. To foil the German efforts, the British also planted mines in the harbors to blow up German vessels. "Everyone," he'd said, "seems interested in our coast."

Marit squatted beside the barely stirring mound. "Oh . . ." Her heart broke. "It's a seal pup!"

The seal wasn't much bigger than a small dog, and it barked weakly, and then made a whimpering, mewling sound.

"We have to help it," Lars said.

The seal pup's coat was black with oil. Its whole face, even its eyes, were filmy. "Run across the pasture to the barn and grab an old blanket . . . there's a moth-eaten one in the loft. Bring that one . . . and I'll wait here. We'll wrap it up and carry it back to the barn. Maybe we can help."

But deep inside, Marit had her doubts.

Lars tore across the pasture.

Left alone with the seal pup, Marit talked to it softly for several minutes. She reached closer and gingerly touched the seal's fur. A sticky black layer clung to her fingertips. She shook her head. "Poor *vesla.*"

"Poor 'little one'?" A deep voice startled her. "What have you found there?"

Marit jumped to her feet.

A lanky soldier with eyes as blue as Mama's stared down at her. How could the enemy look so much like a Norwegian? Around his waist, a leather belt was cinched tightly over his gray-green *jakke.* Along his chest a row of metal buttons sparkled, and above the top right pocket a metal eagle spread its wings.

She lowered her gaze to the seal pup. As angry as she was at Bestefar, she still reminded herself about his warning not to speak to the Germans.

The soldier bent closer and nudged the seal with the toe of his leather boot. The pup whimpered. "Ah, it's not only people who suffer. War has many unexpected casualties."

His manner was official, but beneath the uniform she sensed a human being, if that was possible. Then just as suddenly, he stiffened, as if he just remembered that he was in uniform, and adjusted the rifle on his shoulder. "And what are you doing here on the shore?"

She didn't answer, but glanced back toward Godøy Mountain, a backdrop of lush green that towered above the island's small farms and her grandparents' farmhouse and barn. In the distance across the vibrant green pasture, Aunt Ingeborg hung clothes on the line and seemed to be looking toward them, surely worried.

"You Norwegians. Can't speak a word, can you?"

Like a mountain goat, Lars suddenly sprang over the pasture's edge and onto the rocky shoreline.

"*Halt!*" the soldier shouted, spinning in Lars's direction and drawing the revolver out of his holster.

"*Nei!*" Marit cried.

"Oh, oh." Lars held out the navy wool blanket and froze. His eyes opened wide at the sight of the revolver pointed at him.

"I see you two can speak," the soldier said. Then he pivoted and aimed his gun at the seal pup. "It will die soon enough," he said. "Better to put it out of its misery."

"Please," she begged.

The soldier stepped closer and knelt beside the pup. Marit covered her eyes, bracing herself for the inevitable. Lars began to cry.

Then the soldier stood up and stepped back. "It's dead already. I don't need to waste ammunition." He motioned to Lars with his gun. "You. We need the blanket. It's cold at night. Bring it here," he commanded.

Marit had heard that soldiers often entered houses and "borrowed" whatever they needed. She had a better word for it. *Stealing.*

Lars's lips moved, but nothing came out. He had

frozen in place. The soldier stepped from one boulder to the next until he reached him. He took the blanket from Lars's arms, and then ambled along the breakwater to the lighthouse.

Before anything worse could happen, Marit pushed the rowboat back into the water and motioned for Lars to get in—and quickly. Halfway back to the pier, she stopped rowing and glanced back.

A line of black cormorants flew in formation over the peninsula. Seagulls filled the air with screeching as they circled and landed where the seal pup lay onshore. And in the distance, the soldiers kept a steady watch on the water.

## CHAPTER SEVEN

# Windblown

Marit passed the summer days by scrubbing floors; feeding the goats; cleaning out every corner of the barn; gathering blueberries, lingonberries, and raspberries; and carding wool from neighbors' sheep, which Aunt Ingeborg earned in trade for jars of jam. Only at the general store on mail delivery days did Marit have free time to see Hanna and Olaf, and Kaptain, his growing puppy.

Evenings, they gathered in the kitchen around the radio. Norway's radio station now broadcast only German propaganda. The only news worth listening to was the British airwaves—the BBC. Even though the Nazis forbade listening to it, everyone did. Marit learned that King Haakon had fled the country and was in exile in

London. She was relieved he was safe, but that meant the Germans were now unquestionably in control. What did this mean for Mama and Papa?

Names that had meant nothing to her before now made her shiver. Terboven was one. Vidkun Quisling was the other.

"Quisling—that traitor!" Bestefar nearly spat. "A Norwegian Nazi! How dare he declare that resisting German troops is a crime? He's nothing more than a puppet of the Germans—with Terboven pulling the strings." He mimed a puppeteer pulling strings. "Look at him dance. He thinks he's so clever."

Marit heard speeches by Winston Churchill, England's leader, and by their own exiled king. On the BBC, King Haakon told Norwegians to stand strong and never to give up. His words were immediately printed on illegal presses and spread secretly across Norway.

One day she found a flyer on the road, blown about by the wind, and she read the king's own words over and over:

> *The Norwegian people's freedom and independence is the first command of Norway's Law, and I will follow this commandment . . . the duty given to me by a free people.*

Marit tucked the flyer in her blouse, as if the words were life itself. When a truckload of soldiers approached, the flyer burned against her skin as she pretended casually to pluck and eat the wild lingonberries and raspberries along the roadside. With the truck's gritty dust in her mouth, she ran back straight to the barn.

She passed Big Olga's empty stanchion and climbed the wooden ladder to the hayloft. Flecks of chaff floated in the ray of light from the open loft door. The gray tabby barn cat lay on her side in the corner, nursing five kittens in the straw, her eyes closed as if she didn't know Marit was there.

Marit pulled the flyer out. Such valuable words— words someone had risked his or her life to print and circulate. She couldn't toss them away. She found the loose board, pulled it from its base, and added the king's words to a few shells she'd stashed there years earlier.

The cat opened one eye, watched her, and then closed it again.

A strange mixture of guilt and pride welled in her.

"You saw nothing," Marit said to the cat, which ignored her anyway.

Symbols started to appear around the island. Marit found them scratched in dirt on the road, other times painted over a German sign. The most common symbol was a large *V*, with an *H* in its middle, and a *7* in the middle of that: *Victory for King Haakon VII*. Other times, she found the words "Long live the king" carved or written on road posts and trail posts.

Marit started to wear a paper clip on her collar, just as she had seen others do at the general store. When Aunt Ingeborg asked why she was wearing it, Marit answered, "Mr. Larsen said it's our way of saying 'Let's stick together.'" After that, Aunt Ingeborg started wearing a paper clip, too.

One evening, as they sat listening to the radio, Lars was playing on the living room floor with a tabby barn kitten. "Just for a little bit," he promised, since Aunt Ingeborg refused to keep a cat in the house as a pet. He broke into giggles as the amber tabby pounced on the ball of yarn hidden in the crook of his arm.

Marit watched Lars and wished she could forget about the war as easily.

"What shall I name you?" Lars laughed. The kitten reared back in mock combat, then dashed at the ball of yarn again with his front paws. Lars shrieked with laughter. "You think you're tough, but you're small enough to fit in a teacup!" And it didn't take long before Tekopp, as Lars named him, became a house cat.

One evening, Aunt Ingeborg held a rucksack out to Marit. "Would you bring this to the pier? Bestefar is having engine trouble and he may not make it back for dinner. A little kindness will do him good."

55

Marit studied her feet rather than meet her aunt's eyes. She was reluctant to do Bestefar a favor.

"Marit, I know you and Bestefar don't always agree on things. But he's a good man. I hope you know that. He's extra busy now that the cod season has started. And with the occupation—nothing is normal. Everyone is affected."

For her aunt, she would do anything.

Cheerlessly, Marit crossed the wooden plank to Bestefar's trawler. Harbor currents jostled the boat, even though it was tied up securely with three ropes.

Hands in leather gloves, Bestefar was hammering a poster beside the door of his boat's wheelhouse. He glanced at the bundle she held out to him and nodded.

Marit stepped closer and read the poster aloud. "You shall not in any way give shelter to or aid the enemy. To do so is punishable by death."

"What's that about?"

"Another warning."

With disgust, she watched him hammer the last corner of the poster. Nazis forced their way into their country, and his response was to do everything they demanded. "Bestefar," she asked, her voice shaking with anger, "it says you can't aid the enemy. But *who* is the enemy?"

He avoided her eyes and whispered through dry lips. "Marit, I don't expect you to understand. You're young. If I don't post this, my boat will be confiscated."

"They'd take your boat just because you didn't post the warning?"

He nodded.

"But if every fisherman refused to post it, then the Nazis would have to take every boat . . ."

He studied her.

". . . And soon they'd realize that there weren't any fish coming in to feed their armies. They'd have to let you go back to fishing then, wouldn't they?"

"It's not that simple," he said.

"Bestefar, you didn't even hear me." She'd never spoken so disrespectfully to her elders before. But how could she respect him when he had less backbone than a jellyfish? He made her want to spit on the floor of his deck. "What will they want next? That all the fish you catch raise their little fins and say 'Heil Hitler'?"

He didn't laugh.

And she wasn't joking.

Bestefar's face reddened as he raised one white eyebrow. "Enough. You have spunk, Marit. But remember"— he glanced toward the other boats tied up, as if to see if other fishermen were listening—"you *must* hold your tongue and keep your thoughts to yourself. Do you want something to happen to your brother, your aunt—do you?"

She stormed off his boat deck, knocking a bucket of salt water over in her wake.

## CHAPTER EIGHT

# The *Bunad*

When late-August mornings brought shivers, and yellowing birch leaves signaled the start of school, Marit made up her mind. She had to speak with Aunt Ingeborg. She and Lars had stayed on the island long enough. She refused—absolutely refused—to remain apart from her parents any longer.

Seated at her treadle sewing machine, Aunt Ingeborg worked the foot pedal. The little black machine with small painted flowers stitched rapidly through swaths of black fabric. Already hand-embroidered on the fabric were designs in threads as bright as flowering nasturtiums. Aunt Ingeborg bowed her head over the cloth, her fine eyebrows knit in concentration.

"Aunt Ingeborg, I'm sorry to bother you, but—"

"Good thing I bought all this fabric before the invasion. I've had in mind to start on a *bunad* for you, just as your grandmother did for me and for your mother."

Marit had always looked forward to wearing a *bunad,* the colorfully embroidered black wool vest and skirt with a white blouse worn at confirmation and on special occasions. Boys wore embroidered vests and knickers. Since she could remember she'd looked forward to the tradition. "Thank you, but . . ." Marit said sadly, "but I won't be staying that long."

The entry door creaked and footsteps fell in the kitchen. Bestefar peered into the living room.

"Ingeborg!" he scolded.

The whir of the sewing machine stopped.

"You know the *bunad* is forbidden."

Aunt Ingeborg sat straighter, lifted her chin, and turned to look at him. "In public, Papa, *ja,*" she said, "but those Nazis don't need to see everything we do or wear in private." Her gaze was steady. "Now do they?"

"You could be arrested," he said. "All of us could be."

Her grandfather and aunt stared at each other. Marit knew well enough to keep her mouth shut. The window curtains fluttered in the breeze. Lilting cries of seagulls filtered in with the low mooing of cows.

Then Aunt Ingeborg snapped her gaze away. Her sewing machine began whirring at a feverish pitch. They continued their disagreement the way they usually did—in silence. Marit would rather they kept talking through their differences—the way Mama and Papa did—until they came to some kind of understanding.

"Ingeborg," he said, "I *insist* that you stop work on that. You must hide it or burn it." His fingers tapped at the outer seams of his trousers.

Aunt Ingeborg tucked in wisps of hair at her temple, her chest rising and falling with deep breaths, and said firmly, *"Nei."*

His face reddening, Bestefar shoved his hands in his trouser pockets, took them out again, then turned and went back outside with a huff.

Working her foot pedal into a pleasant whirring, Aunt Ingeborg continued sewing. Marit was amazed that she'd stood up to Bestefar. But more than that, her aunt, in her own way, was standing up to the Germans, too.

Moments passed in silence, then Marit finally remembered the reason she had needed to talk with Aunt Ingeborg. "School's going to start soon, Aunt Ingeborg. Lars and I *need* to return to Isfjorden."

Aunt Ingeborg, two pins held lightly between her teeth, repinned a seam, finished, then looked at Marit with a slow shake of her head. "I don't think you'll return soon."

"But—"

"Marit, your mother and father would have written to tell you to come back by now. It must not be safe."

Marit felt herself crumbling over this—these few words from her aunt that represented so much more. Tears formed at the corners of her eyes. She'd thought that growing up was about being responsible and in control. Now when she wanted things to be different, she had *no* control at all. "We must go to school here, then?" she whispered.

Aunt Ingeborg nodded. "Folks have decided that students will meet at the church building. Church will be held there on Sunday, school will meet there during the week."

Marit had passed the regular schoolhouse everyday on the way to the pier. A large building, the Godøy School had become home to German soldiers and officers. Signs warned passersby not to gather in numbers outside the building.

Aunt Ingeborg's face turned stern, her blue eyes hard. "Do they think our Norwegian children aren't good enough for schooling? That they can just take over school buildings and toss our children on the street? They make me so—ouch!" A tiny drop of blood appeared on her fingertip. Aunt Ingeborg flashed a quick, determined smile as she held up her pricked finger. "The Nazis—it's all *their* fault."

Aunt Ingeborg laughed at her own joke. *Probably her first,* thought Marit. Then she said, "Oh, and I hope you don't mind, Marit, but I'm to be your teacher."

"I don't mind at all." This news softened the blow of not returning home. "But will I call you Aunt Ingeborg or—"

"At school, call me Miss Halversen. But everywhere else, you and Lars are the only ones in the whole world who can call me Aunt Ingeborg." She reached out and touched Marit's hand. "And I wouldn't give up being your aunt for anything in the whole world."

## Chapter Nine

# Iced Out

In September, the Germans ordered that every window be "blacked out" with dark paper so Allied planes would have a harder time hitting German targets at night. The slightest glimmer of light through a blackened window could lead to a knock on the door by the Gestapo—the dreaded Nazi police force.

By day, under the bell tower of the white octagonal church, Marit joined the other fifty-three students. They went from singing "A Mighty Fortress Is Our God" on Sunday to doing math, reading, and language lessons on Monday. At the island's makeshift school, the youngest children sat in the pews on the right, fourth- through seventh-graders met on the left, and the oldest students gathered in the balcony. Even with the war, each grade had to get through its own *pensum,* a series of required subjects.

At first, the teachers—Miss Halversen, her aunt; Mrs. Hammer, who had an irritating habit of tapping her pencil when she corrected papers; and Mr. Moe, who loved to sing louder than anyone in the upper grade—refused to let students wander through the adjoining cemetery. But as the month passed, their rules slackened.

Miss Halversen wore A-line skirts and cardigan sweaters and always started the day with a beaming smile, as if to lift her students' spirits. The smile and cheeriness were something Marit seldom saw at the farmhouse. When Miss Halversen's students finished their lessons early, she let them play board games, spend time outside, or read books of their own choosing. Marit enjoyed this new side of her aunt, as if she were more herself as a teacher than when she was living in the same house with Bestefar.

One day during free time, when Hanna and Marit were leaning against the apple tree, its ruby fruit hanging heavily, Olaf joined them. He sat cross-legged, took his comb from his pocket, and tried to tame the cowlick above his forehead, though it always twisted stubbornly upward as soon as he tucked away his comb.

"How's Kaptain?" Marit asked.

Up close, Olaf's eyes were as smoky gray as low-hanging clouds. "He's coming along. He loves to outrun me, and I'm teaching him to roll over."

Lars came running toward Marit, fell into her lap dramatically, and cried, "Save me, Marit! Save me!"

Two boys circled, sticks drawn like guns.

"Go on," Marit said, and waved them off. They ran away, and Lars bolted after them—stick in hand—around the church.

Hanna wasn't saying a word. Marit curved toward her and raised her eyebrows. "Hanna, are you still here?"

Her friend nodded, and then looked away at the gravestones.

"What's wrong?" Marit pressed. "We're friends. You can tell us."

Hanna refused to answer.

Marit gave Olaf a shrug.

"So what do you think of school here?" Olaf asked her. "I mean, compared to your school in Isfjorden."

"It's different having school at a church, but it's fine. I really like Miss Halversen." She laughed.

"Since you're her niece, she'll probably be easier on you."

"Or harder."

For a few minutes, they talked. He fidgeted with his leather shoelaces, and before long he said goodbye and walked away.

Marit turned to Hanna, whose eyes followed Olaf as

he left them. "Hanna. That was rude. You acted like you didn't even know Olaf. Why wouldn't you talk to him? It's as if he had head lice. I thought you liked him—as a friend, I mean."

"Ice out," she answered.

"What do you mean, 'ice out'?"

"Guess you haven't heard. We have to ice out Olaf Andersen. His parents are NS—the *Nasjonal Samling,* the Norwegian Nazi Party. Marit, they've *sided* with the Nazis." Her eyes narrowed and she whispered, "His parents handed a Norwegian over to the Germans!"

Olaf's parents? Quisling was a traitor, but Marit couldn't believe that any islander, let alone Olaf's own parents, would join the Nazis and turn in other Norwegians. She shuddered. "I can't understand how they . . . but that doesn't make Olaf . . . he wouldn't do that."

"Maybe. Maybe not. It doesn't matter. If anyone in the family is NS, a 'quisling,' then the whole family gets iced out." She nodded toward the tombstones, where Olaf was wandering alone. "It just happened. Yesterday. My parents told me about it last night. By now, most everyone on the island knows."

A wave of cold swept through Marit's body. What if someone turned Mama or Papa over to the Nazis? How could anyone do such a thing? *Why* would anyone do such a thing? Her heart went out to Olaf, but how could she ever understand his parents? "It's like he's dead then?" she asked. "Treated the way we treat the Germans?"

"Sort of like that."

"Like a dog?"

Hanna huffed. "My papa says we try to treat our dogs *much* better."

It seemed cruel, but if "icing out" was a means of uniting against the Nazis, then Marit had no choice but to take part.

After school that day, outside the church gates, steps sounded behind her and someone tapped her shoulder. She spun around, expecting to see Hanna. It was Olaf. His gray eyes were pleading, and for a moment Marit thought he might start crying.

"Listen, Marit," Olaf said, smoothing his hair back with his hand. "I know what Hanna probably told you, but listen—I'm *not* a Nazi. I'm *not* my parents."

Marit felt sorry for him, but in this war—a war in which *her* parents were risking their lives and *his* parents were turning in Norwegians—there was no middle ground. She grabbed her brother's hand and turned away. "Lars, let's go."

She hurried ahead, and Lars kept glancing back. "Why aren't you talking with Olaf?"

"I'll explain later."

That night, instead of cod stew, which seemed to get thinner each night it was served, Aunt Ingeborg served a feast: fish cakes in brown gravy, boiled potatoes, and small pancakes with jam for dessert. Bestefar spoke about his day's catch of herring, and Aunt Ingeborg talked about how the quality of flour was getting worse.

All Marit could think about was Olaf and the haunting words of the soldier on the shore months earlier.

*War has many unexpected casualties.*

## CHAPTER TEN

# If You Breathe

In late September, Marit learned from the radio broadcast that the German leader, Terboven, had stepped in and declared the Norwegian Nazi Party to be the official "New Order" in Norway. There would be no more voting.

One evening, Bestefar brought home a newspaper that was being illegally copied and sent all around the country. Before sharing it, he double-checked to make sure the black paper was tight against all windows.

"If any of us should be asked to trample ideals we cherish," he began reading, looking intently from Marit to Lars to Aunt Ingeborg, "to adopt a new way of life we scorn, there is only one course to take. If this is the New Order, our answer is: No Norwegians for sale. Several hundred Norwegians have sacrificed their lives for something they held sacred. It is also sacred to us."

When he finished, Aunt Ingeborg clapped her hands. "*Ja,* that's right. No Norwegians for sale! Let the Germans hear that loud and clear."

"Unfortunately, the author of these words has been arrested," Bestefar said. "With every day it's becoming clearer. The lines are being drawn. You're either a Nazi or a *jøssing.*"

"A *jøssing?*" Marit asked.

"A loyal Norwegian," he answered quietly.

After that, it seemed almost everyone was a *jøssing.* Even at school, where the red, blue, and white Norwegian flag was replaced with the German swastika flag, little signs of unity sprang up. Along with fishermen, everyone started to wear *nisselues,* red stocking caps like those worn by gnomes. And if not *nisselues,* then they wore red caps, scarves, or sweaters as a sign of unity.

When a German officer stopped by their school, they all pretended to have a scratchy throat and started coughing uncontrollably. Marit had heard that in Ålesund, when a Nazi soldier sat down on a bus, nearby passengers would get up and move to other seats. Nearly everyone, except Bestefar, started sporting a comb sticking out of chest pockets on coats, which meant "we Norwegians can take care of ourselves."

At school, Marit kept an eye on Olaf. Once, she

watched him arrive at the church gate. He paused, pulled a red *nisselue* from under his jacket, and when he thought no one was looking, he donned it. Then he walked around, his stocking cap matching those of the others. It didn't matter. Everyone ignored him. Marit wondered how he could stand coming to school. Many times she wished she could talk with him, but "icing out" was not only a punishment, it was also a warning—a way to remind others to stay loyal. Fair or not, Marit determined she would not cross the invisible line dividing loyal Norwegians from traitors, *jøssings* from *quislings*.

Yet Aunt Ingeborg still talked with Olaf. If he raised his hand, she allowed him to speak. In fact, all three of the schoolteachers spoke with him, one on one.

That evening at dinner, Marit blurted the question. "Aunt Ingeborg, if 'icing out' is a way of reminding everyone to stay loyal, then why do you and the other teachers talk with Olaf?"

Her aunt set down her fork. "Marit, I know it's difficult to understand. But you see, I'm a teacher first and foremost. My job is to teach, to help all students learn, no matter what their family background, their personality, or if they're eager or reluctant to learn. And to do that, I need to treat every student fairly. At school, I cannot 'ice out' Olaf."

"But it's not fair!" Marit said, pushing away from the table. "We were friends, and I *have* to turn my back on him. If I don't, then the 'ice out' doesn't work. I *don't* have a choice."

Bestefar kept eating, but was clearly listening.

Aunt Ingeborg sighed. "But you *do* have a choice, Marit." She reached for Marit's elbow, eased her closer, and then, just as Mama used to do, rested her hand on the small of Marit's back. "There are no easy answers these days. All I know is that you must do what you believe is right—and so must I."

Soon, warnings were posted all around the island, with notices such as "If you remove public notices, you will be severely punished." And the list of warnings grew longer every day:

- IF YOU RISE FROM A SEAT WHEN A GERMAN SITS DOWN, YOU SHALL BE SEVERELY PUNISHED.

- IF YOU WEAR SIGNS OF STANDING WITH THE ENEMY, INCLUDING WEARING PAPER CLIPS, RED HATS . . . YOU SHALL BE SEVERELY PUNISHED.

- IF YOU CLEAR YOUR THROAT WHEN A GERMAN APPROACHES, YOU SHALL BE SEVERELY PUNISHED.

On one such list posted on a dock pier, someone had boldly added in pencil: "If you breathe, you shall be severely punished."

## CHAPTER ELEVEN

# Christmas Eve, 1941
### *One Year Later*

It was Marit's second Christmas Eve on the island, and she felt like a prisoner in her own country. Not only was every window on the island darkened with black paper or fabric, but now anyone caught trying to *escape* Norway would be imprisoned or put to death. This night, more than ever, she missed the cheerful flicker of the season's lights when candles filled everyone's windows.

But not even Nazis had stopped Aunt Ingeborg from preparing for *Juletid*. Since soap was scarce, Marit had helped wash the floors with water and sand. They washed the cotton and lace curtains on the scrub board and hung them to dry. Then they starched, ironed, and put them back up again. Aunt Ingeborg set out bright green, red, and blue table runners, while Lars and Marit polished a few pieces of silver and copper. Together they decorated a pine bush with paper-woven baskets, but this year they would have to skip the tree candles. Candles were too valuable. After the *requisition*—the fancy word the Nazis gave to making every Norwegian turn in their blankets, gum boots, tents, rucksacks, and the like to help the German army—it was surprising that anyone had anything left. Aunt Ingeborg had insisted that the children keep one *dyne* hidden away during the day and take it out only at night. "Paper blankets are not enough to keep children alive in the winter," she'd said angrily.

Unlike other years, when baking had filled the air, they merely talked about their favorite cookies: *sandkaker, krumkake,* and *fattigmann.* Herring and salted cod were stored in the cellar—Bestefar made sure of that—but sugar and white flour were impossible to come by.

"Christmas isn't the same without Mama and Papa," Lars kept saying, as if by saying so he could make them magically appear.

If he said it only their first Christmas apart, it wouldn't have bothered Marit so much. But this year, she couldn't stand it any longer. "Stop!" Marit blurted, turning on him. "If they really cared about us, they wouldn't have sent us away!" Her angry words flew out. "They don't even remember they have children!" She cupped her hand lightly over her mouth. To her own surprise, her words had come seemingly out of nowhere.

Aunt Ingeborg spun around, holding a wooden spoon in the air. It dripped batter. "They sent you away for your safety, Marit. Don't say such things!"

For a few long moments, Marit studied the floor. It seemed that lately every word and thought about Mama and Papa made her angry. Though they'd received a few vaguely worded letters in the past year—it was a comfort that they were alive—it would be so much easier to go through the hardships of war together with her parents than apart from them. If she were a parent, she would never send her children away to be cared for by others. In a time of war, didn't kids need their parents more than ever? And yet, beneath her burst of anger, she really *did* understand that Mama and Papa were doing what they had to do. On Christmas Eve especially, she knew they'd rather be together as a family, too.

"I'm sorry," Marit said quietly, glancing up at her aunt and then at Lars. "I know they care. It's just so hard sometimes."

Her aunt hugged her. "I know."

After Marit bathed with the last bit of soap, Aunt Ingeborg wrapped Marit's hair around narrow strips of paper, just as Mama would have done. That night, with knots all over her head, she struggled to sleep. She wanted Christmas to come, but another year without Mama and Papa made her almost wish away the holiday.

On *Julaften*—Christmas Eve—they sat down after their chores to the traditional dinner of boiled potatoes, brown goat cheese, mashed green peas, and *lutefisk*. Aunt Ingeborg had worked many days soaking the dried cod first in water and then in a lye solution to soften the fish, then in water to remove the lye. The fish filled the house with a nose-pinching odor, worse than Papa's socks after a long day of skiing.

"*Lutefisk* stinks!" Lars complained.

"Wouldn't be *Julaften* without it," Aunt Ingeborg replied.

Even without sweets—or Mama and Papa—Christmas was under way.

After dinner, they put on their cleanest clothes—no new outfits. Not even the *bunad*, which her aunt had apparently lost courage to work on. Marit brushed out her curls and tied her hair with the red taffeta ribbons Aunt Ingeborg had saved for her.

Although *risengrot*—the traditional porridge of white rice, cinnamon, sugar, and a little butter—wouldn't await them after church this year, Aunt Ingeborg had promised them something made out of millet. And whoever found the almond—this year it was a button instead—was assured a good year ahead.

"To church," Bestefar said, and held the door open.

In wool scarves and coats, boots and mittens, they trekked to church, each wearing a required "blackout mark." With the small illuminated tag on their coat lapels, the Germans could see them moving about after the six-o'clock winter curfew.

Nearly everyone on the island was at church and wished one another *"God Jul!"* and sang Christmas hymns. In the back, in a row all by themselves, sat Olaf and his family.

Though Pastor Ecklund's skin was splotchy red and his hair thinning and stringy, his voice was as soothing as dark honey. He spoke about God's love and the gift of sending His son to die for everyone's sins—a message Marit had heard many times before.

As they quietly stepped outside, the stars pierced the sky with a thousand lights. Marit listened to her breath as they walked along the snow-covered road toward home.

Halfway there, a set of car lights suddenly switched on, startling them. They jolted to a stop. Aunt Ingeborg squeezed Marit's shoulder, and Marit clutched Lars's hand.

A car door opened. *"Halt!"*

Marit blinked in the lights' blinding glare, unable to see. A wave of nausea passed through her. Was this to be one of those unexpected arrests she'd heard about? Would they all be hauled away—or shot? She braced herself for the worst possible outcome.

"Marit," Bestefar whispered, "not a word."

He didn't have to warn her. Even if she had wanted to, she wouldn't have been able to speak.

"Identity cards," the soldier ordered.

Aunt Ingeborg and Bestefar reached in their pockets and held out the mandatory identification cards. Anyone fifteen or older who was stopped without identification could be sent to reeducation camps in Norway or Germany—or worse. Executed.

The soldier turned his flashlight on the documents, studied them, and then waved them away.

"And these children?" His flashlight drilled into Marit's eyes, as if the car lights were not enough. Blinded, she looked at the snowy ground. Her hands trembled in her mittens.

"My grandchildren," Bestefar said. "And my daughter Ingeborg's niece and nephew."

"They live here on the island?"

"Ja."

"And their parents? Why are they not with their children on Christmas Eve?"

"They were killed when their village was first bombed."

Marit squeezed Lars's hand tighter, trying to let him

know that Bestefar was telling a lie. Lars squeezed her hand in return.

Like a hound losing the trail of a promising scent, the soldier sniffed, seemingly disappointed. "I see," said the soldier. "On your way then." He snapped a salute, arm extended. *"Heil Hitler!"*

The car rolled on, crunching over snow and abandoning them.

The stars had dimmed and the darkness seemed menacing and endless. Could the Nazis not allow them a moment of peace?

With her heel, Marit carved a large *V* in the road.

## CHAPTER TWELVE

# Miss Halversen's Stand

### *January 1942*

On the first school day in January, Marit watched through a stained glass window as a German officer approached on his black horse. He tied his mount to the gate, then eased open the entry door and slipped into the church. No one else noticed. Marit nudged Hanna, who sat beside her in the pew. "Look!"

His was like all the other uniforms, swaths of gray-green with moving limbs. Marit did her best to ignore them. But she remembered this one. He was the same one who had grabbed Mama's letter and put it in her hand at the general store.

Boots clicked across the floor—six paces—then

stopped. The officer passed his walking stick back and forth from hand to hand. From the back of the church, he watched Miss Halversen as she taught. Her sweaters and skirts curved softly over her tall frame. In the past months, her gray lisle stockings were increasingly ridden with snags. Everything, it seemed, was in shrinking supply or completely gone from store shelves.

After that, the officer started to show up nearly every day, sometimes on horseback, sometimes riding in the side wagon of a motorcycle, at other times in a vehicle, but always just minutes before lunch. Lately, when he visited, Miss Halversen had started to behave oddly. She dropped her pencil. Her hands trembled. She stopped in the middle of the lesson, told them to take out paper, and gave them an assignment. Then she would sit stiff-spined in the front pew beside her pile of textbooks and face the cross above the altar. The officer used to leave when she turned her back to him, but now, more often, he lingered to speak with her during the students' break.

One day, Hanna sat down next to Marit and cupped her hand to her ear. "Maybe he's in love with her."

Just then, Miss Halversen stopped speaking, crossed her arms over her buttoned sweater, and looked at them. "Marit? Hanna? Do you have something you'd like to share with the class?"

Heat surged to Marit's face. This was the first time her

aunt had scolded her like any other student. Along with Hanna, she shook her head and studied the open book in her lap.

In late January, they decided to spy. After lunch, when all the students trailed outside and only the teachers stayed in, they found their chance. The officer hovered in the foyer as students left, and when he was completely focused on Miss Halversen, they crept up the stairs to the empty balcony and ducked down. Marit felt giddy, tucked behind the banister with Hanna. They exchanged smiles. She hadn't done anything this daring in a long time. Her heart pattered as she peered over the top.

"Miss Halversen," the officer said striding up the aisle, his black riding boots gleaming and a small package tucked under his arm. "You look lovely today." His Norwegian was broken. "I must speak with you. Alone."

At the front of the church, Miss Halversen turned hesitantly toward him. Mrs. Hammer and Mr. Moe sat together on the opposite side, going through their lunch tins. Heads together, they appeared lost in their own conversation, though Marit was certain they were listening, too.

"I have told you, *Herr* Schmitz, I will *not* be alone with you."

"Very well," he said, and glanced over his shoulder at the other two teachers, then up toward where Marit and Hanna were hiding. "I would prefer discretion, but if you insist, then let everyone hear, including your two students spying from the balcony."

Marit was aghast at being discovered. She ducked down farther, shoulder to shoulder with Hanna, and froze.

She was sure her heart had stopped beating. What would he do to them? What would Miss Halversen say? She hadn't thought of getting caught. Neither she nor Hanna moved. They weren't going to stand up unless they were asked to. Maybe they could slip back down the stairs and outside before Miss Halversen saw them. But could they get past the Nazi officer?

Miss Halversen stood firm. "May I eat my lunch in peace, please?" Her voice strained with an anger Marit had seen only once at school, and that was when she'd caught Edvarg, the eighth-grader, with his hand in the cupboard. She'd shouted at him for stealing, but when Edvarg said he needed aspirin for his sick mother, she marched back to the cupboard and dropped something into his hand. "Here, leave a little early," she told him. "I hope they help. Next time, ask."

Below them, the officer removed his cap, his short, honey-colored hair combed back in waves. "There's an officers' party tonight. Perhaps you'd care to accompany me?"

Miss Halversen shook her head.

"Other girls and women, up and down the coast," the

officer said, "they've taken German boyfriends. I assure you, it will be all right." He paused, and then continued. "Perhaps a party is the wrong thing. A movie in Ålesund, would that suit you better? I could arrange it. Please." He stepped closer to her, as if to take her hand, but she backed up, out of reach.

"Very well." From under his arm he produced a shiny gold package. "I had to go through some effort to get these, but thought you might enjoy them." He lifted the box's lid, displaying its contents.

"Chocolates?" Miss Halversen's tone was one of disbelief. She looked at the box and then at him. A tremor crossed her face.

Marit's mouth watered. She hadn't tasted chocolate since her last visit with Mama to the milk shop in Isfjorden. Nearly two years! If only Miss Halversen would share the chocolates with her class after the officer left. Or better yet, bring them home to share.

"Everyone is sacrificing," her aunt said angrily. "Even milk is increasingly in short supply. You Nazis take *everything* and leave us nothing. And in the past weeks, many of the children are complaining of hunger." Her voice was quiet but powerful, as if she were holding back an ocean of injustice. "Do you know what it's like to teach when their bellies are rumbling for food? And you bring me *chocolates?*"

She knocked the box from the officer's outstretched hand. Chocolates scattered at his feet. Mrs. Hammer and Mr. Moe gasped, and a disquieting hush fell over the church.

Marit covered her mouth.

As if stunned, the officer didn't move. Then, almost in slow motion, he took two steps back. He snapped his officer's cap on his head and straightened his jacket. When he spoke, his voice was sharp. "You could be arrested for such talk," he warned. "I was trying to court you. I could have forced you, but I didn't. I'm doing you a favor."

Miss Halversen stood tall.

The officer turned away. His heels hit sharply across the floor, echoing stonily through the church building, and the door shut hard behind him.

As soon as he was gone, Mr. Moe hurried to Miss Halversen. "I can't believe you knocked the gift from his hand! You're so brave, Ingeborg."

"Or impossibly stupid," muttered Mrs. Hammer, her arms crossed squarely. "He'll make us pay for this, you can count on it."

Miss Halversen dropped to the pew and bowed her head in her hands. Her shoulders rose and fell with silent sobs. If she hadn't been spying, Marit would have rushed down and put her arms around her.

Hanna nudged her in the side and motioned toward

the stairs. Stealthily, Marit crept down the stairs after her. Once outside, they ducked snowballs, passed snow forts, and wandered through the gravestones without talking. A chill far colder than the winter air settled deep in Marit's bones. With her mitten, she swept the wind-blown snow off the headstones, as if learning the dates of every birth and death was more interesting than talking with Hanna about what had just happened to Miss Halversen.

## CHAPTER THIRTEEN

# Unspoken Thoughts

On February 1, 1942, Marit celebrated her twelfth birthday. Hanna came over for dinner and gave Marit a pair of multicolored wool mittens. "I knit them out of yarn from old socks."

The thumbs were a little lumpy, but to Marit they were the best gift in the world. "They're beautiful! *Tusen takk!*"

Lars gave her a tiny wooden gnome roughly carved out of wood. It wore a tall pointed hat—that much Marit could make out—and had two feet.

"Lars, for being only eight years old—"

"Almost nine. Only two months away," he reminded her. "April second, remember?"

"Right. Almost nine. You're an excellent carver!"

That night, as Lars drifted to sleep, she lay awake in the complete darkness of her bedroom. Another year had passed. Did her parents think of her and wish they could be with her on her twelfth birthday? If they were alive, she knew they would. Mama used to make *lefse,* Marit's favorite, and sprinkle the rolled potato pancakes with butter and cinnamon. After every birthday dinner, Papa always took out his Hardanger fiddle. With it rested under his chin, he'd tap his foot along with "Two Mountain Trolls" until she and Mama and Lars started dancing on the wood floor.

Months had passed since Mama and Papa's last letter. They had sent a letter every three months. Marit suspected they would write more often if they could, but that they didn't want to attract any extra attention that would in any way connect their efforts in Isfjorden with their children on the island. If one family member was found helping with the Resistance, the whole family was usually killed.

Still, they were due for a letter soon. As each third month arrived, the wait for their letter became unbearable, her worries torture. If Olaf's parents could side with the Nazis, then there had to be others, too. What if her parents had been reported by a neighbor for helping the Resistance? If arrested, they would face torture, re-education camps, or death. She wanted to believe that

Norwegians were quietly winning the war through underground methods. But were they? With each passing day, ordinary people seemed to lose more of their freedoms.

She whispered again to herself, "Mama and Papa are fine." Teardrops fell from the corners of her eyes and into her ears. She didn't bother to wipe them away.

Later that month, icy winds turned to gales as Marit walked with Aunt Ingeborg and Lars to church, their heads bent into the wind. Bestefar, who usually didn't miss a service, was away fishing for a few days.

Pastor Ecklund stood before his congregation. His usually blotchy red face was as pale as a peeled potato. He clung to the edges of his simple podium, as if to hold himself upright. His normally long-winded sermon ended abruptly. For a long moment he was silent, and when he started again, his voice carried determination.

"My dear friends, this will be my last service here. Bishops and pastors across Norway have decided to resign their posts, and I am resigning as well, as a matter of conscience. We will not be under the Nazis' authority—only God's. And I cannot in good faith lead you if I must bear a Nazi yoke."

A rush of whispering swept through the church, but Pastor Ecklund raised his hand, bringing quiet again.

"To agree to partner with the Nazis would mean to be puppets in their service. They would approve or disapprove of sermons. They would command us how and what to teach. And I know it would not be a message of God's love, forgiveness, and goodwill toward others. It would be to further their cause of racism, fear, and intimidation. Services here will henceforth be led by Nazi-appointed pastors. I will, therefore, not meet in this building," he said. "Rather, I invite you all to join with me in worshiping in the privacy of our homes."

Over the next week, snow fell and blew into drifts around the church building. During breaks at school, Marit and Hanna often took shelter from the wind in a snow fort they'd carved from a deep drift. The half roof and short walls glowed an icy blue and protected their secrets.

Marit clapped her birthday mittens together to warm herself. The sun barely traveled above the horizon, casting long shadows from the gravestones across the snow. From her squatting position, she rose to stretch. The wind, damp from the sea and stiff with cold, slapped her cheeks. She ducked back down, but not before spotting Olaf wandering toward their shelter, his stocking-capped head tucked between his shoulders.

"Olaf. He's coming this way. Do you think he wants to talk to us?"

Hanna shrugged and rubbed her mittened hands together.

In seconds, he was standing there. Wind teased the tufts of sandy hair jutting from his cap. He shifted from boot to boot, his gray eyes downcast.

"Marit, I must talk with you."

She looked at Hanna, whose eyes were determined, reminding Marit of their unspoken decision. Marit wished things were different. They rose in unison from behind their snow wall and walked away.

"I feel bad for him," Marit said under her breath. "Terrible—but we have no choice."

"I know," Hanna replied. "We have to."

That afternoon, before Miss Halversen excused them for the rest of the day, she stood in front of all the students. First, she called toward the balcony, then to the younger students. "I'm speaking for all of the teachers here at Godøy School," she began, a history book clasped against her yellow sweater. "We want you to know that teachers across Norway have been ordered to teach students Nazi propaganda." She paused, as if to make sure they had heard.

Marit couldn't imagine it. Miss Halversen was supposed to teach them how to be Nazis?

"Teachers across Norway are united. We have sent in

countless letters *refusing* to instruct our students in Nazi thinking. And do you know what Nazi philosophy is?" She didn't wait for an answer. "It means believing that you are of a superior race—an Aryan race—superior to anyone who is of Jewish ancestry, superior to anyone who is handicapped or different in any way. It means teaching you to identify and pick out those who don't fit in. It means that you are to follow orders and obey and not to ever, *ever* think for yourselves. We cannot and will not obey this request by the Nazi authorities. To do so goes against our training and conscience as teachers. We're Norwegians. We believe in the God-given worth of every individual. We believe in freedoms for everyone."

The students, like still treetops before an ominous storm, didn't move.

She inhaled sharply, then continued. "We don't know what will happen next. And so, I wanted to warn you. If anything should happen to teachers, should any of us suddenly disappear or be replaced, you will know the real reason. For now, teachers across Norway stand together."

*Teachers disappearing or replaced.* Marit's mind teetered at the edge of a possibility she hadn't considered. Would the Nazis stop at nothing? Marit drew a *V* in her notebook and followed the lines with her pencil—over and over until the paper ripped.

She was sick with worry for her goodhearted aunt.

That night, Aunt Ingeborg added corrections to a stack of papers. With school under way, she didn't have as much free time to knit or sew. Bestefar's disapproval must have stopped her from working on the *bunad*. Or maybe when she considered the risk of getting caught, she decided the *bunad* wasn't worth the price of Gestapo punishment.

Seated by the wood stove, like a tailor with an oversize needle, Bestefar pushed a metal fid through strands of thick rope, creating a loop for a mooring line. "For the teachers to openly defy the Nazis," he said, "it will cost many lives. The Nazis do not tolerate disobedience." He flashed Aunt Ingeborg a look of grave concern.

Her reply was resolute silence.

"But Bestefar," Marit said, taken aback by his response. "Don't you understand how brave the teachers are?"

He looked at her, but his blue irises were as unreadable as the sea, and his lips were closed maddeningly tight.

Of course he didn't understand! And now in his tight-mouthed way, he wouldn't say another word on the subject. She found her rucksack and settled at the table to do her homework. As she opened her mathematics book, the numbers on the page blurred. Her thoughts wandered, but slowly came into alarming focus.

In the past year, Bestefar had worked increasingly long nights. Once, he had been at sea for over a week. While he was gone, Aunt Ingeborg spent more time than ever embroidering the *bunad,* and often her eyes were red from fatigue.

"When will Bestefar return?" Lars asked after six days of their grandfather's absence.

Aunt Ingeborg cast her gaze beyond them. "Fishermen. They have minds of their own." That was all she would say on the subject.

Increasingly, though Marit hated to even think it to herself, Bestefar seemed less and less a *jøssing*—and more and more a *quisling*.

In mid-February, as welcome as the winter sun climbing above the eastern peaks, another letter finally arrived— three and a half months since the last one. Bestefar read it aloud. Like the previous letters, this one was written in Mama's hand, but signed Mr. and Mrs. Siversen.

> *Dear Ingeborg and Leif,*
> *Months have passed and our hearts break with missing you, our most precious friends. You're lucky to have the company of grandchildren to help you on your farm. We hope they're a blessing to you.*

*Our work continues. Very difficult, but making prog-
ress. We trust the Lord to help us and everyone these
days. Difficult times, yet the mountains are as beautiful
as ever.*

*Hope your fishing is successful, despite the dangerous
activities at sea these days.*

*Hearty Greetings!*
*Mr. and Mrs. Siversen*

It wasn't much, but Marit clung to the words of the
letter, repeating them over and over to herself until she
had memorized them. Every night, Marit repeated the
letter to herself before asking the Lord to keep Mama
and Papa safe. And every morning, on her walk to the
church for school, she recited the letter in her head, trying to stretch the meaning of each sentence, trying to
hear Mama's voice in every word.

## Chapter Fourteen

# Distant Dreams

"Marit," Aunt Ingeborg called upstairs, "before you get dressed, try this on."

Lars was already up and feeding the chickens. But this morning, Marit was in slow motion. She didn't feel like getting dressed. Despite the recent letter, she didn't want to be helpful. Every chore was set against a hopeless, gray backdrop of never seeing her parents again, of a world where war never ends. In her nightgown, Marit peered from the top of the stairs.

Draped across Aunt Ingeborg's arms, brilliant threads of blue, red, and orange joined in flowers and swirls across the black fabric of the *bunad*. "Surprise!"

"Oh," Marit said, reaching for the *bunad*. "You finished it! I thought you had given up."

A smile flickered over Aunt Ingeborg's face before her stern expression returned. Marit knew her aunt was pleased but didn't want to appear boastful of her handiwork. Then she handed Marit a white blouse, a pair of silver-buckled black shoes, and red anklets.

Marit was stunned. "This is too much. When did you work on it? Where did you get—"

Aunt Ingeborg waved her concerns away. "I had a little savings. I worked on it when I couldn't sleep. We must *never* let some traditions die. And the *bunad* is much more than just clothing. Sorry it took me so long."

In no time, Marit slipped the white blouse over her head, pulled on the vest and skirt of the *bunad,* and adjusted the front ties. It *was* more than clothing. This particular embroidered design and style had been passed down from the Sunnmore region, east of Ålesund, and home of her ancestors. *Bunads* were worn with pride at every important event and celebration. She smiled as she pulled on the socks—red in color, because she wasn't married, of course—and then the shiny buckled shoes, which had been worn before but had recently been buffed to a high polish with cod liver oil, the only oil to be found.

Marit twirled until her skirt billowed.

She touched the neck of her blouse. A round *sølje* with dangly silver—that was all that was needed to make her *bunad* complete. Some things were too expensive, too much to hope for. She hardly recognized herself in the mirror. She saw less of the girl she had been in Isfjorden and—in the rise of her cheekbones, the set of her jaw, the arch of her eyebrows—more of Mama.

"Marit!" Aunt Ingeborg called up. "Are you going to take all day to show me how it fits?"

Embarrassed, Marit hurried down the stairs.

Aunt Ingeborg nodded. "Now turn around. It suits you and fits well, with plenty of room for you to grow. Now you'll have it to wear for your confirmation and for special events."

Though Marit knew she could never wear the *bunad* in public, she twirled again, too happy to contain herself. If Bestefar had been home, she wouldn't have dared to try it on, but he had left early and was fishing already, despite the pale rising sun of winter.

"Pack it away, Marit, in the chest in your room. Hide it at the bottom, underneath everything else, just to be safe."

Marit started up the stairs, then turned back and threw her arms around her aunt's neck. "*Tusen takk,* Aunt Ingeborg!"

That night by the radio, Aunt Ingeborg and Marit exchanged glances, sharing their own secret. Bestefar didn't need to know that the *bunad* was done. Let him worry about something else. When Aunt Ingeborg finished correcting assignments, she took skeins of undyed wool. "Lars, you need a bigger sweater. Dyes are impossible to get these days, but at least sheep are still in abundance on the island."

The radio crackled. Marit wondered why Bestefar listened so closely if he didn't believe in standing up to the Germans. These days, he spoke less and less.

The king's voice came in clearly for a moment. "All for Norway," she heard, but his words faded in and out. How long could Norway stay strong without their king, without more help from the Allies? Many German warships had been bombed by the Resistance when they entered Norwegian harbors, but the Nazis were always quick to react—sometimes burning whole villages in response. Hanna had complained that just that week Nazis had visited their house in the middle of the night without so much as a knock. They slammed open the door with the butts of their rifles. "I don't know what they were looking for," she said. "But when they took the one good piece of soap that my mama had hidden in a drawer, she couldn't stop crying for a long time."

## CHAPTER FIFTEEN

# New Orders

On March 20, a ray of sun fell perfectly on Miss Halversen, backlighting her golden hair. But this afternoon, her forehead was etched with lines, her mouth tight and strained, and her skin pale. "We have been informed," she announced to all the students, "that schools across Norway are to shut down for one month due to a 'fuel shortage.'" She moved her lips, as if to say more or to explain this strange statement to them. Instead, her eyes flitted to the back of the church.

Marit turned and her heart caught. She elbowed Hanna. "Look!"

The officer who had tried to win their teacher's affection hadn't been around for a year. Now at the back of the church, he towered in his uniform. She hadn't heard him arrive. The sun glinted off the eagle pin on his jacket and shot needle rays around the church. At his heels waited two younger soldiers, both armed.

"*Fräulein* Halversen," the officer said from the back of the church, as if he didn't dare get too close to her. "Come with us."

"You must all be brave," Miss Halversen blurted, rushing headlong with her words as the soldiers marched toward her. "Remember, you are Norwegians. You must be brave—and wise."

Within seconds, the two soldiers grabbed Miss Halversen by her arms. "I'm capable of walking on my own," she said. They released their hold, and walked on either side of her.

Whispers fluttered around the room. The soldiers looked neither left nor right, but straight ahead to the foyer, and Miss Halversen walked with them. Marit felt the blood drain from her whole body. She wanted to shout out, to tell them to stop. They couldn't take her aunt away! But along with everyone else, fear tethered her to her seat and sealed her lips. The moment they stepped out of the church, Marit jumped from her pew toward the open door, and the rest of the students followed her lead, pressing in around her.

She stared. The soldiers pointed to the back of an empty army truck, their breaths forming white clouds as

 AVON PUBLIC LIBRARY
BOX 977/200 BENCHMARK RD.
AVON, CO 81620

they spoke. Without allowing her to take a hat or winter *jakke*, Miss Halversen—her own aunt—climbed in and sat on a bench.

The officer slipped into the back of the other vehicle, a sleek four-door car. Through the window, Marit watched him nod to the driver. The car gunned gravel, and the truck careened after it down the sloping road toward the harbor. From the rear of the covered truck, Miss Halversen stared back at the school, lifting her pale hand in silent farewell.

*"Nei! Nei! Nei!"* Marit wailed, her legs threatening to buckle beneath her. "They can't take her! They can't! That's my aunt Ingeborg! They can't!" But the truck was already gone.

A firm hand grasped her shoulder and tugged her backward. "Marit, Marit, come. Children, children. Inside now," ordered Mrs. Hammer. "Come, sit down."

A blizzard of thoughts and feelings left her numb as Marit walked blindly to her seat. Mrs. Hammer shored her up with an arm around her waist, steering her toward the pews at the front of the church. Marit slumped into the pew as Mrs. Hammer stood before the altar. "Quickly now. The rest of you—take your seats."

When everyone was seated, she explained. "This *is* terrible. I'm frightened and upset, too. We heard rumors that *one in ten* teachers would be rounded up across Norway and sent to concentration camps in our country. Now we know it's true. The Nazis want to scare us into obeying. They want us to bend to their ways." Her voice broke. "Now, go home and pray. Pray every single day for Miss Halversen and for teachers across Norway."

As other students gathered their things to leave school, Marit grabbed her *jakke* and rucksack and raced out to find Bestefar. Lars would have to catch up with her. Bestefar had to find some way to get Aunt Ingeborg back! She had to tell him what had happened.

Breathless, she arrived at his boathouse. But he wasn't there. And his fishing trawler was gone from the bay.

When Lars caught up with her on the road, Marit couldn't speak. In the past two years, with constant worries about the war, Marit had leaned on Aunt Ingeborg. Her kindness. *Her being there.* She'd become more than an aunt. She was like her second mother. Hot tears ran down her cold face. She wiped her nose on the sleeve of her *jakke.* Everyone she loved was being taken from her.

"Marit," Lars said, his voice wavery. Marit noticed his mittens were clumped with snow. "Aunt Ingeborg will come back," he said, patting her arm. "You'll see."

That night, when Bestefar stepped into the farmhouse, he went right past the thin soup on the stove that Marit had made and turned on the radio.

"I heard what happened," he said, spinning the knob until the BBC came in fairly clearly.

Marit listened intently to learn about the Nazi round-up of teachers across the country. The news went from bad to horrible. Not only were teachers sent to concentration camps for "reeducation" but also, to set an example, five hundred of the one thousand arrested teachers were crammed into the hold of a boat and sent from Trondheim up the frigid northern coast.

Bestefar raked his hand through his hair. "The *Skjaerstad* is a small coastal steamer—meant to carry one hundred fifty or so passengers—not five hundred!" His eyes were rimmed red and Marit was sure he'd been crying. "Ingeborg! How could they take her from us? What's becoming of the world when good teachers like my Ingeborg can be treated like livestock?" Head bowed, he said, "God protect her."

That night, before bed, Marit stopped at the threshold of her aunt's upstairs bedroom. It was tidy. Her sheepskin slippers were lined up neatly under her bathrobe, which hung from a peg beside the door. On her pine dresser, her pewter set—hand mirror, comb, and hairbrush—waited for her return. Marit considered sleeping in her aunt's bed. She wouldn't have to share with Lars.

But she couldn't. That would be the same as saying her aunt would never come back. Besides, only a large sheet of paper draped her aunt's mattress. After the requisitioning of all blankets, the only warm covering in the house was the *dyne* that she and Lars slept under every night. Before bedtime, they always pulled it out from under their mattress, shook it hard to fluff up its feathers, then hid it again in the morning. Marit turned away from the doorway. Without Aunt Ingeborg, the house felt cold and hollow.

After that day, Bestefar fell into a rock-hard silence. The cooking and cleaning fell to Marit. Lars tried to help, but he was better at tending the goats and chickens. When he tried to cook, he made more of a mess than it was worth.

Over and over Marit replayed the image of her aunt being taken away, trying to imagine if there was something she could have done to stop the soldiers. With dread, she thought of Aunt Ingeborg being tortured. Or being crammed with other teachers like slaves into a crowded boat. Marit couldn't help but scan the sea, wondering if brave teachers were out there, floating through mine-laden waters. Though the hours of daylight were lengthening, the darkness over Norway seemed only to deepen. Bestefar said he would try to find out what he could about Aunt Ingeborg, but as no news of her whereabouts came, the week passed like a year.

The morning the "donation" truck pulled up to the barn, Marit watched from the window, hiding behind the curtains. The soldier read something to Bestefar from a piece of paper, and then left with his milk and eggs.

Stepping inside, Bestefar brushed white flecks of snow from the shoulders of his wool jacket and sat down heavily at the table.

Marit stopped sweeping. "What is it this time?"

He rubbed his forehead with the back of his hand until his skin turned red as crab legs. "All radios must be turned in by the end of the day. This evening, they will do a house-to-house search. Anyone caught with a radio will face a firing squad."

Lars sat cross-legged on the living room floor holding Tekopp. He looked up, his eyes blank, then returned to playing with his cat. Without the radio, they would not hear any news from Britain. No news about teachers or other efforts by Norwegians—like Mama and Papa. Bestefar's radio was their lifeline to the outside world. It meant hope. He simply couldn't give it up.

"Bestefar, what will we do?" Marit asked. "Hide it?"

He circled his hands around an empty coffee cup and answered in a faraway voice. "I must turn it in. The price is too high."

The broom she'd been clenching dropped from her hands and clattered on the floor. Her eyes filled with tears. She could never know for sure what her own Mama and Papa were doing. But she believed they had sent their own children away so that they might work actively against the Nazi occupation. Her own aunt Ingeborg, her own teacher, had stood up and refused to do as the Nazis commanded and instruct students in Nazi propaganda. She'd risked her life on it—and now she was somewhere, probably in a reeducation camp. Yet Bestefar sat there, playing it safe, unwilling to take a chance on a hidden radio.

She yanked on her boots and tore her *jakke* and hat from the wooden peg by the door. She couldn't stand to be in the same room as her grandfather. Without thought as to where she would head, she stomped out and turned northeast.

Past several narrow farms and along a footpath that wove up the hills, Marit ran and ran. The top of Godøy Mountain called to her, and maybe she was angry enough to keep going until she had reached the top. The past month had brought rains and snow, leaving a thin crust of snow-covered ice over the path. She stomped through it, gulping the damp air as she slowed to a walk. It wasn't safe to be alone, a girl in the woods. But she didn't care. Nothing was safe anymore. School wasn't safe. Not even Aunt Ingeborg had been safe.

The path was familiar and brought back memories. Once at Lake Alnesvatnet on the top of the mountain, she'd caught her first trout, its scales iridescent as it flip-flopped on the shore.

An irritable cawing sounded overhead. Two ravens sat in the top branches of snow-laced cedars. Marit passed beneath them, ignoring their squawking complaints and fluffing of feathers.

At the next clearing, she stopped and looked back. Godøy and the surrounding islands rose like humpback whales from the sparkling sea. Sun glinted off distant peaks and melted the snow into icy waterfalls and streams that emptied into the ocean. So much had remained the same. The same sea, the same deeply carved fjords, the same towering mountains beyond. Nearly two years had passed since she'd last returned home from skiing in the mountains with her family—two long years since bombs fell and her world collapsed.

Marit pushed on, keeping the coast in sight. At the base of a low-sweeping cedar, something red caught her eye. She stopped. At first she thought it was a pine grosbeak with its fluff of rosy-red feathers, but a shiver went through her. It wasn't a bird at all, but a spot of blood.

Had a rabbit or squirrel been caught by a predator? An owl or wolverine or lynx? Stepping closer to investigate, she saw no signs of a struggle. No paw prints from a preying animal. No feathering of wings in the snow from a hawk or owl. Fresh snow from last night covered everything.

She inhaled sharply, looked closer, and saw that the blood extended under the thick branches. Her stomach lurched. She tripped backwards, away from the tree and whatever might be lying in its shadows. Suddenly the distance between this lonely place and the farmhouse seemed enormous.

Through the cedar's low branches, a man whispered, "Don't move."

## CHAPTER SIXTEEN

# A Desperate Plea

*Run,* her instincts told her, but she froze. If this were a Nazi commanding her to stop, the price of fleeing would be death. Yet something about the voice . . . This man's Norwegian was perfect, not the broken Norwegian of a German soldier.

"Please," he said, a desperate plea rather than his earlier command. She couldn't see movement beneath the tree's branches. The man was well concealed. She expected to see the barrel of a gun pointed toward her.

"Please," he repeated. "Help me."

Marit opened her mouth, but her throat had gone dry.

Branches rustled and a gloved hand pushed away the lowest snow-covered branch. A man rose up on his elbow from the ground, just enough for her to see his face. "I'm N-n-norwegian." Beneath a navy wool cap, just like Bestefar's, his cheeks were tinged white from frostbite. As he spoke, his teeth chattered. Certain now that he was in no condition to harm her, Marit pressed closer so she could better make out his words. As she did, he flopped back, groaned, and disappeared beneath the branches.

With a quick glance around to make sure no one was coming up the path from behind her, Marit pushed the branches aside and gasped. The man's right leg ended in a mass of mangled leather and flesh. Above his injured foot, a leather belt was cinched tight around his shredded and bloody pants leg.

"Oh—what happened to you?"

"They shot . . . our boat. Sank us."

"Us? Who?"

"Resistance. F-f-ive of us," he stammered through bluish gray lips.

"And the others? Where are they now?"

His nostrils flared and he looked away.

She couldn't get involved. *Turn. Run away now.* If he was indeed a Resistance fighter and the Germans found her helping him, Marit would be taken away. Perhaps Lars, too. "I need to go home."

The man opened his eyes. "I've been here . . . since . . . since last night. Help me . . . finish."

"Finish what? What do you need to finish?"

"Mission—f-for Norway."

Every moment that she lingered drew her into his fate. And if she helped him, she would be putting not only herself at great risk. Stories she'd heard from the islanders flashed through her mind. Whole families removed in the middle of the night, whole villages bombed beyond recognition, simply because one person was caught helping the Resistance. She remembered the warning posted on Bestefar's boat: "You shall not in any way give shelter to or aid the enemy. To do so is punishable by death."

Marit shook her head. "*Nei*, I'm sorry. I can't. I can't. It's too dangerous."

Trembling, she backed onto the path, turned, and began retracing her steps. Sunlight glinted off the sea and snow-crested mountains, piercing her eyes. She stopped. If she left him, he would die. If she helped him, others' lives would be at risk. She remembered Pastor Ecklund's pale face when he chose to step down from the pulpit, and his words: "We will not be under the Nazis' authority—only God's."

Her own words to Bestefar taunted her. "If no one fights back, then what will happen?" How easy it was to accuse Bestefar of being cowardly. How easy words were!

She could almost taste the bitterness of risk.

In war, nothing was simple.

Head down, she studied her leather boots and her red

wool socks protruding through the toe holes. Another reminder of the war. With leather so difficult to come by, she hadn't been able to replace the boots she'd outgrown. She'd cut the holes so her toes had a little more room. It was either that or Aunt Ingeborg's jam money to buy boots made from fish skin, and Marit had refused to let her aunt waste her money on such things. "I would rather wait until times get better," Marit had said. And when would that be if Norwegians didn't fight back? Her toes were damp from the melting snow and turning numb with cold. If her toes were cold, he must be nearly frozen.

The path wound down at an angle in the direction of the farm, but from where she stood, the ocean was only a stone's toss away. Below her, the rocky beach was empty. The man was badly wounded, and she doubted he could walk all the way to the road. If he could slide down the short slope to the water below, she might be able to meet him and row him somewhere safer.

With a deep breath, Marit turned.

Snow crunched beneath her boots as she headed uphill again to the soldier. She scanned the empty trail, pushed back a cedar branch and found him.

His eyes were half-closed and his breaths rose and fell in wheezes. Frost lined his jacket collar and the rim of his cap. If his boat was shot at, then he must have swum to shore and climbed here.

Marit cleared her throat, hoping to draw his attention. "How can I help?"

He didn't answer.

She knelt closer to his shoulder until the branches swooped back over her, hiding them both. She kept her eyes on his face, trying to avoid his mangled foot. She tapped his chest. No answer. She tapped him again. "I'll help you, but you must tell me what to do."

He lay there, unresponsive.

First, she needed to get him warm. But how would she move him? She would ask Bestefar. *Nei.* She shook her head. He'd likely report the Resistance soldier to the Nazi headquarters—just to play it safe.

Marit considered her options. She could hide the man somewhere near the farm and tend to him in secret until he recovered. The root cellar, or the loft, perhaps. But she couldn't possibly move him by herself. Hanna? Maybe she could help. But then Marit would be involving her friend and putting Hanna's whole family at risk as well.

With the force of breaking ice on a water trough, she thumped the man's chest. "You must—wake—up!"

He moaned. *"Mor . . ."*

"No, I'm not your mother. And I'm going to need your help."

She removed her mittens, reached for his closest hand, worked off his frozen, bloodstained gloves, then placed his icy hand between her warm bare hands. His teeth began chattering again. After a time she put his hand back in his glove and placed her palms on either side of his face and held them there until his eyes opened in panic. "Compass," he said, "I need . . . to get—"

"First, you have to survive. Now sit up. Can you do that?"

Face contorted, he rose to his elbow. Marit felt horrible, for making him suffer more pain. "Can you get down the hill to the shore?" She pointed at an angle to where the distance between the tree and water was shortest. "You could lie on your back and slide down much of the way."

He nodded, but his eyes were glassy and distant.

Marit was formulating a plan as she talked, and tried to sound confident so he'd trust her. "The sun will be down soon, in less than an hour. There's a house-to-house search going on for radios sometime today, so I doubt the waters will be watched as closely. If you can manage to get yourself down to the water, I could row by—"

"You'd attract at-t-t . . ."

"Attention?" She shook her head. "I don't think so. I've been rowing before. The soldiers at the lighthouse don't even see me anymore. Just be there. Somehow, I'll help you to a place where you can hide. You'll have to crawl a short distance to the barn."

He answered by shutting his eyes. His life, it appeared, was a skiff drifting farther and farther out to sea.

"Don't die on me! I can't carry you, and I refuse to get anyone else involved. Just be there, near the shore, just after the sun sets. You'll have to climb in the rowboat. I'll bring a *dyne* to cover you."

"*Dyne?*"

"*Ja.*"

"Warm."

"That's right." Marit peeked out through the branches. The trail was free of other hikers. She slipped back onto the path and started toward home, behaving as naturally as she could, trying to calm her flurry of emotions. She hoped no one would notice her tracks, but there was no way to hide them now. She would steal the rowboat from the boathouse, row past the lighthouse as the shadows deepened, and meet this wounded soldier on the shore.

If he was there.

She would wait no longer than a minute. One minute —she'd count it out—and not a second longer. After that, if he wasn't there, she would be forced to leave him to his own fate.

## CHAPTER SEVENTEEN

# The *Kraken*

Marit shouldered the farmhouse door, and removing her mittens, headed straight to the washbasin. Her bloodstained hands tinted the water pink.

"You're back!" Lars said, skipping from the living room.

Marit glanced over her shoulder.

Under his arm, Lars carried Tekopp, who by now was far larger than his namesake and struggled to break free.

"Where were you? You were gone so long! Bestefar wasn't happy that you were gone."

"I had to take a walk, that's all." She deftly dumped the washbasin water down the drain and dried her hands on a towel.

A pot sat on the cookstove and the room was filled with the smell of cod, thinned milk, and potatoes. Marit lifted the lid. "Bestefar made stew?" she whispered, amazed.

"*Ja,* and I helped cut the potatoes," Lars said, hands on his hips. "We ate already."

"Huh. And Aunt Ingeborg thought he couldn't cook for himself."

"Don't worry. She'll be back, Marit."

Her heart stuck in her throat. "I'm sure she will."

At the smells, Marit's stomach grumbled. But the soldier must be far hungrier. And he needed something hot in his belly. If she could manage to hide him, then she could sneak warm food to him. She ladled a bowl of soup for herself, sat down, and ate quickly.

"You shouldn't hike alone," Lars said. "That's what Bestefar says."

She had no time for small talk.

"He said it's dangerous with so many soldiers on the island."

Marit refused to meet his eyes. If Bestefar only knew. "Where is he?" she asked.

"Fishing. He said he'd be back before dark."

"I-I want to row before it gets dark, too."

Lars slid in his socks across the wood floor.

"Careful," Marit warned. "You might get a sliver."

"Marit," he said and slid again, "I want to go, too."

"*Nei,* Lars. You stay here. Take care of Tekopp."

He planted himself in the center of the kitchen and crossed his arms over his chest. His chin puckered. Marit knew the look. "Marit," he said, holding his voice firm, "please!"

Marit moved to the kitchen window, eased back an edge of the room-darkening paper, and gazed outside. The sun was low. She must leave soon, before her grandfather returned. She struggled to think up an excuse to keep Lars from coming along. "It's pretty cold, Lars. Are you sure?"

"I've been inside all afternoon. Aunt Ingeborg always said it's good to get fresh air."

She pushed the paper back in place. "All right then—a short trip before it gets dark. There's safety in numbers, right? Isn't that what she said, too?" Marit told him in a rush, pushing away from the table.

He smiled and nodded vigorously.

She was uncertain about the outcome, but she was forced to take Lars along. "Let's go!" Before they passed the barn, Marit had an idea. "Let's get that wool blanket from the loft."

"But the soldier took it, remember?" He scrunched up his face at her as if she'd lost her mind.

"The soldier? Oh, right. The German soldier at the lighthouse . . ."

Her mind was tangled. Too many lines in the water.

"Besides, why do we need a blanket?" Lars asked. "Did you find another seal pup?"

She thought of the Resistance soldier. Hardly a seal pup. "No," she said. "To help you keep warm."

He shook his head vigorously and stood taller. "I'm fine. I won't get cold. I'm not a baby, Marit. I don't need a blanket."

"Oh, no, I was thinking, um, for Tekopp. Maybe he wants to go for a boat ride with us. You could go find him and bring him along. He'd like that, don't you think?"

His eyes widened. Without a word, he ran back to the house and returned with Tekopp, wrapped up in their puffy *dyne*. "Aunt Ingeborg wouldn't want this outside."

"I know. We'll be careful."

The Resistance soldier would be a fool to climb into a rescue boat with two kids and a cat. But she had promised she'd be there. She had no choice, and she doubted he had other choices.

In the lengthening shadows, they headed down the road to the boathouse.

To Marit's relief, Bestefar's trawler had not yet returned. She poked her head into his boathouse and was met with the smells of oil, decaying rope, old barrels, and fish. Assured that her grandfather was nowhere near, Marit stepped to the rowboat.

The sun shot a fireball of red across the water. Marit breathed in deeply, hoping for courage, then she lifted the rowboat's bow and pushed. The stern eased onto the water as she held the bow. "Climb in."

Carefully, with his overly bundled cat, Lars crawled over the middle seat to the stern, a big smile on his face. "Let's be Vikings! Let's hunt down the *kraken*!"

"Why would we want to find a sea monster?" Marit asked, hoping to keep his mind occupied.

"We could tame it. Make it our pet! And then it would protect us, even when Mama and Papa are far away." Perched on his seat, with the *dyne* covering his knees, Lars snuggled his face into Tekopp's amber fur.

"Sure," Marit said. "We can pretend."

The water glittered dark with rubies as Marit rowed. They headed from the harbor to the lighthouse, but this time she kept rowing past the end of the peninsula. Two German soldiers huddled beside the lighthouse, out of the wind, their cigarettes glowing.

One of them looked up as they rowed past. He must have decided they looked harmless, and shaped carefree smoke rings that floated up, circle after circle, and disappeared in the air.

"Marit," Lars whispered, "we're not supposed to go past the breakwater. Are we really looking for sea monsters?"

"We are."

Off toward the open water, porpoises arced, diving in and out of the gray waves. "See them?" she asked.

As Lars turned, the porpoises skimmed the surface, dived, and were gone. His jaw slackened. "Sea monsters!" he whispered, with enough awe in his voice that Marit didn't know if he was playing along or truly believing in impossible creatures.

"*Ja,*" Marit said, leaning toward him. "And they may have injured a Viking long ago somewhere along the coast. If we find someone, we must be very quiet and help him."

"A Viking?"

Marit nodded. "He may not look like a Viking. They don't always wear their metal helmets or carry long swords. But he would speak Norwegian, just like us."

"Keep watch, Tekopp," Lars said, "a Viking."

Beneath the water, boulders lay visible and some broke from the water. Marit rowed closer to shore, careful to avoid rocks that could rip open the bottom of their wooden boat or hold it fast in place like a beached sea turtle. They rounded a bend and reached the beach where trees met the shoreline.

Marit began to sing aloud, "Oh, Viking, Viking, where are you?"

Lars looked at her with an expression of wonder and respect.

Rowing parallel to the shore, well beyond the lighthouse and its guards, Marit sang out again, "Oh, Viking, Viking, where are you?"

A flock of oystercatchers worked the beach, poking their orange pencil beaks in and out of crevices. Again she sang out and glided forward. A few of the birds, their black-and-white feathers sharply contrasting with the gray light, scuttled away from her approaching boat.

A haze of movement caught her attention. Onshore, easing from behind a boulder, the injured Resistance soldier stumbled toward them, his face milky white. Bent nearly in half, he hobbled toward the water with the use of a stout stick.

Lars gasped but—thankfully—didn't scream. "Marit! He's hurt!"

"Don't say a word," Marit ordered. "That's our Viking . . . injured many years ago by the *kraken,* and now we must rescue him."

Lars stared at the creature hobbling toward their boat. "He doesn't look big enough to be a Viking."

"Well, not all Vikings are huge."

Marit rowed quickly—pull, pull, pull—until the bow just touched the shore. The soldier tumbled headfirst into the boat with a grunt, and then curled into a ball on the floor between them.

"We must hide him," she said.

Lars put Tekopp beside him on the seat, and then spread the *dyne* over the soldier. "His foot. He's hurt bad," he whispered.

"*Ja,*" Marit replied. "And we must keep him a secret."

Marit studied the mound and looked at Lars. This wouldn't work. If they rowed back like this, the soldiers would know they'd picked up something, or *somebody,* along the way. How stupid could she be? Why had she ever agreed to help?

"Lars, the *kraken* is still searching for this Viking—and for little boys—to gobble up. And right now, it's very important that you hide under the *dyne,* too."

He made a face and shook his head. *"Nei."*

"Don't worry, this man won't hurt you."

Lars pulled in his lower lip, a sign he was getting ready to debate.

"I'm serious, Lars!" she cried, and then tried to act less demanding. "Please," she begged in a softer voice, "do as I ask, and if anyone stops us, don't say a word. Pretend you're sleeping."

Reluctantly, with Tekopp, he crawled under the edge of the *dyne* and disappeared. The mound at the bottom of the boat was large, but Marit hoped it would go unnoticed.

Then, with a silent prayer for their safety, she began rowing back. The rowing was harder now, and though the breeze had died, the sea worked against her in swells. She pulled her elbows back against the darkening waters. Sweat formed on the back of her neck and down her spine. As she neared the lighthouse, she glanced over her shoulder to stay on course. She didn't want to get closer to the lighthouse than necessary, but she didn't want a current to sweep her farther out into the bay, either.

"*Fräulein,* where is your brother?" a soldier called out, startling her to her toes. Marit recognized his voice. He was the German soldier who had come to investigate the seal pup onshore. She hadn't expected the soldiers at the lighthouse to think it was out of the ordinary for her to be rowing. His question unnerved her, but she forced herself to remain calm.

She let go of the oars, pointed to the mound at her feet, and bent her head against folded hands, hoping he would get her silent message.

The soldier nodded. "Oh, sleeping!"

She nodded and returned to rowing, but the guard held up his hand and motioned to the cove beside the breakwater. "Stop. No farther tonight."

Marit held the oars above the water. Her heart stopped.

"Soldiers are searching the island. You could get shot on the water. Pull your boat to shore and walk home from here."

So that was why he'd commanded her to stop. Her heart started beating again. She knew she couldn't argue. She pointed the boat into the cove. Would he come and take the *dyne*? Her plan to help the Resistance soldier was unraveling. She was a fool, and not only had she put herself in danger, but now she risked her brother's life and the Resistance soldier's, too. It was just a matter of moments before they would all be found out. She was practically delivering the wounded soldier into Nazi hands.

The boat nudged against the shore. The sun had set, and shadows and darkness merged. Shaking, sweat running along her spine, she climbed from the bow and with more strength than she knew she possessed, pulled the weighted boat onto the shoreline.

At the lighthouse, the German soldier faced the shore, watching them.

"Come, Lars," she said, pretending to shake him awake. "Climb out of the boat." He emerged, his face full of questions. She held her forefinger to her lips.

A risky idea came to her. Extremely risky, but the only thing she could think of. Earlier, the soldier had said they needed more blankets. If she could distract him, then the wounded soldier might have a chance to escape without being seen.

"Lars, wait here by the boat for me. And don't say a word."

Lars nodded, with Tekopp nestled under his chin.

Marit pulled the *dyne* off the wounded soldier, whose eyes widened in alarm. She whispered, "In a moment, I'll distract the guards at the lighthouse. When I do, head north to the pasture. You'll see the barn and you can hide in the loft. It's dark enough—they may not see you cross the field." Then she pointed with her head toward the barn. At first he didn't move. Had he lost his hearing? If he couldn't get out of the boat, then what was she to do?

To her relief, he nodded.

"I'll meet you there when I can," she said, then turned to Lars. "Wait here for me."

"But Marit—it's getting dark!" With the situation so confusing and alarming, perhaps that's all he could think to say.

She gave him a kiss on the top of his head, something Mama would have done to reassure him. "I'll be right back."

The fluffy *dyne* filled her arms and she carried it along the shore, across the narrow cement breakwater—careful not to slip into the freezing waters on either side—all the way out to the lighthouse where the two soldiers watched. With each step, her legs weakened. Was she walking into her own trap? She wanted to run and get away from the soldiers, but she willed herself to slow down and walk calmly—stretching out time as much as possible to help the Norwegian soldier escape. Her whole being quaked, yet Marit held out the offering. She hoped that it wouldn't be bloodstained from the soldier's wounds. That might lead to another round of questions. She forced an outer calmness and vowed to keep her mouth shut. Not a word.

The Nazi soldiers stepped toward her. The one who

earlier had aimed at the seal pup took the blanket and smiled. "Eiderdown!" he exclaimed. Then he continued in rough Norwegian. "For us?"

Marit nodded, and then lowered her eyes.

"The Gestapo," he said, and pointed toward the farmhouse.

What? What could he mean?

"They're gone now," he said. "It's safe. You can come back for your boat in the morning."

She almost felt she could trust him.

He lifted the blanket again and smiled. *"Tusen takk."* She was turning to leave when he held up his hand in command.

A panic filled her. Had he figured out her scheme? Did he know that she was trying to create a distraction? She studied his face and tried to read his meaning.

He removed his glove, reached into his jacket pocket, pulled out two chocolate hearts—the kind Papa used to buy her at the milk shop in Isfjorden—and patted them into the palm of her mitten. She stared at them, not sure how to respond. He chuckled as he turned away.

Again, Marit forced herself to walk casually—rather than sprint—back along the wall to the shore. As she looked back, her German soldier had rounded the lighthouse, the *dyne* wrapped around his shoulders. Another soldier said something in German, and they laughed. Perhaps they thought the *dyne* was a real gift, that she was in love with them; or that she was feeling guilty about not having turned it in earlier; or that she was thanking him for warning her about rowing farther. Or perhaps they laughed at the simple mind of a Norwegian girl giving up something so valuable.

With Tekopp in his arms, Lars waited beside the boat, thankfully now empty. Darkness nearly swallowed it whole. Marit pulled the boat higher onto the shore, tied the bowline around a boulder, and hoped it would hold when the tide rose. The lighthouse sat eerily dark, permanently turned off now so that Allied ships and planes could not see the island.

Clouds hung low and covered the evening sky, eclipsing moonlight and starlight. Tekopp meowed, and Lars put him down and let him run free. As they crunched over snow patches in the pasture, Marit kept watching for the wounded soldier. She reached into her pocket.

"Here," she said, handing Lars a chocolate. She popped the other chocolate in her mouth, startled by its unexpected sweetness. Marit reached for Lars's mittened hand and kept walking. "You did a good job," she said.

He squeezed her hand. *"Takk."*

"But Marit, why did he sneak away?" he whispered.

"I don't know."

"Vikings fight—they're not afraid of anything. Not even the Nazis."

"No more talk," she said. "Remember. It's our secret."

129

Tekopp pounced on anything that moved as they crossed the field. The injured soldier was nowhere in sight. Her stomach rolled with nausea as she thought of the risks she'd just taken, of what she might have set in motion. She put one foot in front of the other and kept walking. In spite of Gestapo orders to darken every window, a sliver of light escaped from the farmhouse— enough to guide them.

## CHAPTER EIGHTEEN

# In Hiding

When they slipped into the farmhouse, Bestefar had not yet returned. Without the *dyne* to cover them, Marit and Lars slept with sweaters on over their pajamas and two pairs of wool socks each. In the middle of the night, Lars tapped Marit on her shoulder. "Marit?"

"*Ja?*"

"I'm freezing."

The damp chill of March had crept into their bed, clung with icy fingers, and refused to let go. Marit hadn't slept either. "Me, too," she said. "Follow me."

Quietly, they slipped downstairs and put on their *jakkes,* mittens, and hats. She debated about putting on her boots and going out to the barn to see if the soldier had made it there, but she didn't dare open the door, which creaked worse than an old mast in the wind. She'd have to wait until morning. Tiptoeing, they climbed back upstairs and curled up, back to back.

"Marit," Lars whispered in her ear.

She cupped her hand over his ear in return. *"Ja?"*

"Where's the Viking?"

"I hope he made it to the loft. I'll check in the morning."

"Let's check now."

She had to admit, that was exactly what she wanted to do. But if she waited until just after dawn, Bestefar would be gone. "Better to wait. And remember—"

"I know, you've told me a thousand times. Not a word."

"That's right. You know, you're pretty smart, Lars."

"I know. That's what Bestefar tells me."

Before the sun rose, Marit was in the kitchen, pulling on her boots to milk Big Olga.

"You're an early riser today," Bestefar said, startling her. He stepped from his adjoining bedroom, pulling his suspenders up over his shoulders. Ashen half-moons lay beneath his hollowed eyes. He was growing thinner, and the arrest of Aunt Ingeborg—his daughter—appeared to be wearing on him. "Already dressed and ready for chores, I see."

"*Ja,*" she replied and headed out.

Big Olga stomped her foot when Marit entered; she was clearly not in the mood to wait. Marit would milk her first, and then search for the soldier. She listened for sounds of movement above her or from the corners of the barn but heard nothing.

In the warmth of the barn, surrounded by the comforting smells of manure and animal sweat, Marit sat on the wooden stool beside Big Olga. Tied in her stanchion, the cow chewed hay and stood still for Marit as she worked. *Ting, ting, ting.* The foamy milk hit the side of the metal bucket. Aunt Ingeborg had taught her how to milk when she was quite little. As the milk rose in the bucket, steam gathered around Marit's bare hands. The barn cat strolled in, a new batch of barn kittens racing ahead of her. Marit angled one of Big Olga's teats and shot a small stream in their direction. They pawed and licked at the air, catching a bit of the milk on their tongues. Such generosity. War made sharing even a few drops of milk an extravagance.

When Marit finished, Big Olga craned her neck and looked back at her with grateful brown eyes. Marit poured the fresh milk into the milk can, then patted Big Olga's neck before turning her out with the other cows.

The German soldiers had started weighing the milk on a scale when they came to collect their "donation."

And Marit knew she shouldn't remove even a cupful of what they expected. But today she would take a chance. With a wooden ladle, she scooped out some milk, and then put the cover back on the pail. She would add an equal amount of water to the container later, and hope that the soldiers couldn't tell the difference. Stealing from the Germans. It felt good.

Carefully keeping the ladle upright, she scaled the ladder one-handed to the loft, praying that the soldier had found his way there. She pulled herself to the loft floor and scanned expectantly. He was nowhere to be seen. The cats, in hot pursuit of the scent of fresh milk, scaled the ladder after her and began purring and winding their way in and out of Marit's legs.

"Sorry," she said. "Not for you this time."

A mound in the corner rustled with movement. Fully buried beneath the straw, the soldier lifted his head, his skin colorless and his hair tangled with straw.

*"God morgen,"* she said, trying to sound like Mama on the icy mornings when Marit hadn't wanted to get out of a warm bed. She knelt next to him with the ladle of fresh milk and pushed away the eager barn cats.

He eyed the milk hungrily and reached for it, his hands trembling so hard Marit thought he might spill every drop.

"Here," she said, "let me." She brought the milk to his

chalky lips. Greedily, he gulped the milk down. Then he dropped back into the straw. "And water," he said. "I'm so thirsty."

"*Ja,*" she said. "I'll get some."

Rather than bring water from the hand pump in the kitchen, which was risky, Marit scooped a bucket of water from the animals' trough outside. A thin covering of ice was already melting in the early rays. Though snow stayed for a long time on the mountain, the island's farmlands rarely froze over, and the snow usually melted within days of falling.

The soldier drank three ladles of water before he said, "Enough."

"That's good," she said, trying to sound cheery. "Before long, I'll bring you something to eat, too."

"*Takk,*" he said, and burrowed beneath the straw again without another word.

When Marit entered the kitchen, Bestefar was busy ladling porridge from the cast-iron pot into bowls. "Marit," he said, his voice serious. "I just went upstairs to wake Lars, and your *dyne* is missing. Missing!"

Marit's heart dropped. She had hoped to come up with an excuse for its disappearance, but she was too late. Pinpricks shot through her. Could Bestefar read the guilt on her face? "I know. I should have told you."

Lars sat at the table, spoon in hand. Marit stared at

him, hoping to remind him that he wasn't to say a word about the soldier—or Viking.

"And that's why you came downstairs fully dressed this morning?"

She nodded.

"And you and Lars slept in your hats and *jakkes*?"

That part was true, too. "*Ja,*" she said quietly.

"They're worse than lice!" he growled.

Marit wasn't sure what he was talking about. She remembered how much Aunt Ingeborg hated lice, how she had treated and combed the heads of two school kids to help them get rid of the pests. But that was last fall—months ago. What was Bestefar talking about?

"Yesterday," he said, "when I returned briefly from fishing, soldiers were here at the house. You two were gone. They told me, 'Enemies on the island' as they jabbed pitchforks in the hay, tapped on walls, and even searched upstairs. And then they stole your *dyne*! Wasn't it enough to requisition all our blankets last fall? They say they need *everything* for their soldiers fighting throughout Europe and Russia. We held back only one. Only one! *How* do they expect children to stay warm? They are heartless!"

Marit breathed out relief. Her deception was covered by the Nazis themselves. *Let them take the blame.*

After breakfast, just as Aunt Ingeborg would have done, Marit and Lars washed clothes and sheets on the washboard and hung them on the line to freeze-dry in the breeze. When a quiet moment came and Bestefar was gone, she sneaked out with Lars to the barn.

They'd both saved a bit of their breakfast porridge and a little cheese for the soldier.

"How come you're so young," Lars asked the soldier as he ate the food with his hands, "when you've lived so long? Are you really a Viking that the sea monsters hurt?"

The soldier looked at him quizzically.

Marit nodded encouragingly.

"It's a secret," he said, his hands trembling. A deep crimson brightened his cheeks. Marit touched her hand to his forehead, as Mama had done to her so many times, and felt the soldier's fever travel through her fingers.

"You're burning up. You must rest."

He finished the small bit of food, and then lay back again.

"What's your name?"

"Henrik."

"We'll let you rest then, Henrik." She started to her feet as Lars climbed down the ladder.

"Wait." The soldier's face was guarded.

Marit couldn't see his face; he was hidden so completely. Only his arm stretched through the straw, a metal compass dangling in his hand. "I can't make it. You must take this to the fishing village—north side of the island. I was to have landed there."

The village he spoke of boasted the largest lighthouse on Godøy and was not an easy jaunt down the road. It would take a full day of hiking to get there and back—or a boat ride halfway around the island.

"But why?"

"No—no questions. The less you know, the better."

She remembered Papa telling her the same thing. She reached for the compass, and as soon as she lifted it from his hand, his arm flopped down beside him, as if he'd been holding a great weight. He lay there, his arm in full view. Marit covered it with straw again and leaned closer.

"Who . . . who do I take this to at the fishing village?"

"First house in the village," the soldier said, struggling for air between phrases. "Farthest house from the lighthouse. Ask for Astrid. Say, 'Do you have any klipfish for sale?'"

"Klipfish?"

"*Ja.*"

Then she repeated his instructions back to him.

"Good," he said. "And when she asks you how many, you say, 'A bucketful.' And make sure you show her an empty bucket. Can you remember this?"

"Astrid and klipfish," she repeated. "And I must bring an empty bucket."

"*Ja,* that's good. Go . . . please," Henrik whispered from beneath the straw, "before it's too late."

And then he was silent, completely hidden and completely still. Marit left him and joined Lars below. She held the compass in her hand. Lars scooted closer. "What's that for, Marit?"

"For telling direction. North, south, east, or west." She didn't want to involve Lars in this, but she would look more suspicious acting on her own. And she would risk a scolding and too many questions from Bestefar if she left Lars behind. It was early in the day. If she took off with Lars, they would appear as two bored kids trying to fill their unexpected days off with something to do. With school temporarily shut down, this would seem believable.

Marit paused, reminding herself of the risk, another choice filled with *unthinkable* consequences. She'd heard stories about the Gestapo: the woman who had her fingernails pulled out, the fisherman from Ålesund taken away for questioning and returned with cigarette burns across his body, the numerous bodies found floating in the sea ... Norwegians ... and no one knew what terrible things they'd suffered before drowning.

Compass in hand, her palms slippery with sweat, she examined the silver object and the simple carving of a ship on its cover. She flipped open the lid, expecting to find a note, a piece of paper, something secretive. But it looked like an ordinary compass. She turned toward Godøy Mountain and the needle pointed north. It worked like an ordinary compass. What could possibly be so important about it that this man, Henrik, would travel the sea, have his boat shot out from under him, lose his companions, and entrust her with it? There had to be more to it.

Marit forced a smile and feigned enthusiasm. "Lars," she whispered, "are you ready for another adventure?"

## CHAPTER NINETEEN

# A Bucket of Klipfish

Though the hike over the island's peak to the fishing village on the other side was daunting, Marit thought she could make it. She was less certain about Lars, especially if they ran into snow at the top. And she doubted he'd be strong enough to hike back again. Unlike Papa, she certainly wasn't going to carry him over her shoulder if he got too tired. That left only one other choice. They would row to the island's north side.

Marit packed a chunk of cheese, two slices of coarse bread, and a jar of water. Over their *jakkes*, they pulled on dark, canvas raincoats. Marit sniffed. *"Uff da!"* Bestefar had bought the raincoats for them in Ålesund, but they were not soaked in regular linseed oil, which had disappeared; these raincoats reeked of cod liver oil. Putrid smelling—but better than nothing in such weather.

A light drizzle misted the air. Shades of deep gray blanketed the sky above the sea and pasture. They hiked toward the lighthouse shore where the rowboat waited, nudged higher onshore from tidal currents.

"Help me push," Marit said, throwing her weight against the bow.

Lars's face reddened as they edged the boat slowly over the kelp-covered rocks. From the corner of her eye, Marit saw a German soldier trot across the breakwater toward them, gun over his shoulder.

The compass around her neck turned weighty as an anchor.

*"Hei! God morgen!"* he called with a wave.

Marit froze.

In a few long strides, the soldier was at the boat's side, pushing alongside her. Marit looked at him questioningly, and he smiled in return. It was the soldier she'd given the *dyne* to yesterday. She could not understand his motivation, but inside, she breathed a prayer of gratitude.

Within seconds, the boat eased into the water. Fast as rabbits into their burrow, she and Lars slipped into the safety of the rowboat. Lars sat in the bow so he could look ahead; Marit sat in the middle seat, facing their wake as she rowed. With a wave, she thanked the soldier, and then pulling quickly on the oars, glided away from shore.

She'd come to feel completely at ease in the rowboat, the oars familiar in her hands—the only thing left in life over which she had control. The task of rowing to the north side of the island would not be easy. She pulled hard, stroke by stroke, and they rounded the lighthouse and peninsula and skimmed over boulders that lay dangerously close to the surface.

"Keep a lookout for sea monsters," Marit called, just in case the soldiers could hear. "We're off on another adventure!"

Lars gazed at Ålesund to the east. Marit hoped that Bestefar's trawler was nowhere in sight. He would be furious to see them go beyond the lighthouse boundary, and he'd stop them.

To blend in and be less visible from the water, Marit kept the rowboat close to shore. If she strayed too far, they could end up wrestling ocean currents. Fortunately, morning waters were fairly calm. The rowboat crested over the tops of small waves and pulsed them toward the northeastern point of the island. The shoreline drifted by quickly. They passed farms, a single red boathouse, the wooded shoreline where she'd found Henrik, and another pasture where sheep grazed on patches of last year's grasses. Snows had begun to melt.

Drizzle drenched her face, but Marit didn't mind.

Perhaps this mission would be easy to accomplish after all. With a breeze at their stern, they glided easily. She understood the risk, but to be doing something to help the Resistance was exhilarating. For two years she had not been able to do anything to help fight the Nazis. Just a week ago, she'd stood mute and helpless as Nazis hauled her aunt away. Finally, she was doing *something*.

Unlike Bestefar, she chose to fight back.

"Are sea monsters related to trolls?" Lars asked, keeping watch.

"No, sea monsters live in the ocean. And trolls, they live deep in the mountains. They're all scary, but no, I don't think they're related."

"And they eat children."

"Oh, I don't think trolls like the taste of children. But they sure like mountain goats." She glanced over her shoulder at him, not sure if he really believed in such things anymore. Either way, at least he was willing to play along.

"Oh," Lars said, sucking on his lower lip. "And Henrik, did he really hurt his leg by fighting the *kraken*?"

"*Ja,* he's very brave."

"But then why did he hide from the soldiers in our barn?"

"Sometimes Vikings get hurt and they need to heal before they can go back to battle."

"Did the *kraken* bite his foot?"

She nodded.

"Marit," he said, his dimples forming tiny crevices in his rounded cheeks. "Are you telling me the truth? Are there really sea monsters and trolls? Is he really a Viking? Are you sure? Do you swear on the Bible?"

She drew a breath. This wasn't the time to tell him the truth. If she just played along, she lessened the risks for him should they be stopped and questioned. She remembered Papa's words: *The less you know the better.* In war, she now understood, this was often true.

"Lars," she said, "this is serious. Just keep a lookout. Better to keep watch."

That was all it took. Lars turned his gaze back to the sea, ready to resume his post. Marit was relieved. She needed to have him work with her, even if he didn't know the real reasons why.

She rowed on. Drizzle soon turned to plump raindrops. Her thoughts drifted with the current. She wondered about her old friend Liv. What was she doing at this moment? Marit pictured her on a distant farm, helping with chores, maybe reading a book in the hayloft in a patch of sunshine. Liv loved to read.

At the most eastern point of the island, their luck changed. Waves struck boulders and sent sheets of white spray into the air. Marit rowed hard as they veered into a wind that swept toward the island's rocky northern shore. She leaned hard into the oars.

"Watch for boulders!" she called.

"But I can barely see," Lars whined. "I'm getting rain in my eyes."

"Try!" she shouted. "I don't want to look over my shoulder and lose ground. Call out, 'keep left' or 'keep right.' Help keep us headed toward that lighthouse ahead. Do you see it?"

"*Ja!* Red and white striped."

"Good."

Only a fool would try to row into the wind here. But she *was* a fool, just like her Papa. If Bestefar thought such heroic actions were foolish, then let him. She pulled harder against the oars, straining her back against the bitter wind.

Icy salt water sprayed over the bow, pelting the back of her slicker. Lars whined. "Marit! We should turn back," he called. "I'm scared."

"If we make it to the village, then the sea monsters will be afraid of us. Right now, they're stirring up the waves. They're trying to scare us away from our mission! Be brave!"

Gasping for breath, lungs and throat on fire from the effort, Marit heaved on the oars, stroke after stroke after stroke. Her shoulders pinched in painful knots. Despite sprays of freezing water, she removed her mittens to get a better grip on the oars' handles. Blisters formed and soon broke in the crook of her thumbs, and she winced with each splash of salt water. She tried to think beyond her pain. Think of Aunt Ingeborg, she told herself, who might now be in a "reeducation" camp, or crammed with other teachers in a boat, journeying up the coast as a mine finder for the German boats that followed behind. This was one of the rumors she had heard. Think of Henrik, wounded and feverish in the hayloft, just because he was trying to help Norway. Marit clenched against the pain, against the burning of her muscles, and against the Nazi occupation—and rowed all the harder.

Abruptly, the shore rose to steep cliffs. If Marit couldn't hold them on course, the waves would seize their little rowboat and toss it against the rocks the same way seagulls drop clams to crack their shells.

Under a sky of slate drizzle, minutes turned to endless hours. Wave by wave, spray by spray over their bow, they began to take in water. Marit checked over her shoulder, uncertain that her raw and blistered hands would hold out much longer, but ahead—to her relief—two break-waters beckoned like arms and offered protective harbor. She kept rowing.

As they drew closer, she looked again. A lighthouse towered above a slope dotted with sheep and houses of red, green, and gold and a row of boathouses perched on the shore. Through the mist, two German trucks traversed the road toward the lighthouse.

The rowboat finally rounded the breakwater. The

waves settled. A sea otter slid off a rock, floated on his back, then dived.

"See that?" Lars said.

Marit rowed past docks, where a fisherman, head bowed under his rain hat, unloaded lobster creels from his boat to the docks, but he paid them no attention.

"Lars, you need to wait here and watch the boat. Eat the cheese and bread we brought. Maybe that otter will show up again. Keep watch, Lars, and I'll be back soon. I promise."

She jumped from the boat, tied it up, and left Lars. The compass was tucked safely next to her chest, and beneath it, her heart pounded like a trawler's engine. She passed idle nets and strings of small fish drying beneath boathouse eaves. Under her breath, Marit repeated Henrik's instructions. "'Do you have any klipfish for sale?' When she asks you how many, say, 'a bucketful.'"

With haste, she headed beyond the boathouses to the first house on the edge of the village—a white house trimmed green. It was closest to the harbor, and farthest from the lighthouse that towered above the fishing village. It had to be the one.

Darting across the muddy road, Marit turned into the yard. With its stone foundation and slate-covered roof, the house was ordinary. Nothing about it hinted at Resistance activity. Had she remembered the instructions?

She swallowed hard, marched up to the door, and knocked.

Footsteps pattered inside, then paused. Finally, the door edged open.

Through the crack, a man with an unshaven face and the expression of a tombstone stared at her. One of his thick arms hung in a sling. If he was trying to discourage visitors, his manner was definitely working.

"I-I thought a woman lived here. I'm sorry." She turned to leave.

"What do you want?" he demanded.

Halfway down the steps, Marit turned. Could she trust this man? It was the right house, she was sure of it. But wasn't she to meet with a woman? Had something gone wrong? "Is Astrid here?" she finally asked.

The man didn't answer for some time. Finally, his voice softened.

"*Ja.* Do you have a message for her?"

Was she to wait for a woman to appear or carry on with her part? But the man knew the name, and maybe that was enough. She plowed ahead. "Does she have any cod—" She caught herself. "I mean, klipfish for sale?"

"I see. And what will you carry it in?"

"Oh, no! Wait, I can go back to my rowboat. I have a bailing bucket."

His face showed no expression as he waited for something more.

"I need a bucketful," she stated firmly.

He nodded. "And in return for klipfish?"

Her fingers trembled as she reached inside the top of her sweater and found the compass and its chain. She removed it from around her neck and handed it to the man.

He glanced at its cover. *"Ja,"* he said. "This will do. *Tusen takk,"* he added, then turned away and closed the door behind him.

Marit stood there, alone on the doorstep, bewildered. Was there more she was expected to do? Had she completed her part of a code? Should she have something in exchange to take back to Henrik—klipfish or something to prove that she'd done as he'd asked? But the door remained closed.

The man's message to her became clear: *Leave. And leave quickly.*

## CHAPTER TWENTY

# Ancient Walls

**A** truck rolled past Marit, splattering her with puddles of freezing mud. In the back of the truck, German soldiers huddled under a canvas top, heads down, shoulders hunched in the cold. Beneath her raincoat, she shook violently. Eyes lowered, she kicked at a clump of melting ice that lingered at the edge of the road and waited till the truck bumped away before she moved.

In the rain, she sprinted across the road and along the breakwater, hoping Lars had stayed put as she'd asked.

"I saw the otter again," he said, his voice wobbly, his face ashen. Was he chilled to the bone?

"Good," she replied. She fumbled with the lines, and finally untied them. Then she jumped in and took up the oars. The faster she could get them back to the farm-house, the better.

The wind had kicked up small whitecaps in the sheltered harbor. It would be much easier returning with the wind at their backs on this side of the island. Her shoulders tensed as she eased past a couple of fishing trawlers. Two fishermen watched her with curiosity. She didn't have klipfish to show them. And no good excuse for being there, either. She hadn't thought that far ahead.

Pulling against the oars, she nudged the bow past the breakwater walls and into open water. As soon as they passed the sheltering cement arms, a wave slammed up against their stern and pushed them forward. They rode swiftly up the crest of a frothy wave, slipped down to its base, then rushed ahead to the top of the next swell.

Wind hissed in Marit's ears and stung her face. Her vision blurred with sheets of raindrops and salt water. Still, with her oars in the water, she held the rowboat steady and kept its bow pointed straight into the waves. A slight twist or turn, left or right, could tempt a wave to reach out and swamp them. She couldn't risk that. She also couldn't leave guiding the boat to Lars's judgment, so she kept glancing over her shoulder to make sure the bow was cutting straight through the powerful waves. In no time at all, they approached the farthest edge of Godøy. Somehow, she'd have to cut quickly to the island's eastern point, but the waves had grown wild.

"I'm getting sick," Lars moaned above the wind. "I can't stand going up and down!"

"Put your head between your knees," she offered, without turning to look at him. "Maybe that will help."

"Nooo," he wailed. "That makes it worse."

"Try looking out and breathing lots of fresh air! If you get sick, use this." She skipped a beat with her oars, grabbed the metal pail at her feet, and tossed it over her shoulder to Lars behind her at the bow. Rowing again, she shouted, "Don't lean over the side! I don't want to lose you!"

Suddenly, out of the corner of her eye, Marit saw him. He was on his feet, wobbling, and he tottered toward the edge of the boat.

"Lars, no! Sit down!"

She let go of the oars, jumped forward, and pulled Lars back to his seat. He held the bucket between his knees. Head down, he retched.

Marit slid back on her seat and glanced around. One moment, that's all it took. They'd gone too far past the calmer lee of the island. They'd lost their only chance to cut south. Instead of heading home, they had been pushed by large, deep rollers northeastward—straight for Giske Island.

*Nei! Nei! Nei!*" Marit protested against the power of the wind and current. She had no choice but to row with the cresting waves, to do what she could to prevent them from turning sideways. They were in open water, rushing headlong to the nearest island. She let the waves push them toward Giske. When the winds died down, she'd row them back to Godøy.

Lars finished using the bucket and looked around. "Marit!" he screamed, his eyes wide with fear. "Floating mines, remember?! What are you doing out this far?"

"This wasn't planned!" she shouted. "I didn't *try* to get us out here. If you hadn't gotten sick—" And then she stopped herself. That wasn't fair. He didn't need her yelling. It wasn't his fault—or hers—that they were adrift.

"I'm sorry," she said, looking over her shoulder to Lars. "I'm sorry you don't feel well. Are you better?"

He nodded, though his skin matched the greenish gray of the sky.

"Keep a lookout for anything floating that could be a mine."

She expected him to whine, but he didn't. He perched on the bow seat like a carved figurehead on a Viking ship's prow. They drifted on.

"There, on the right!" he said, and Marit veered the oars and shifted the boat to the left slightly. "No it's not—it's a killer whale!"

Marit shot a glance over her shoulder. "Oh, my!"

The head of a black and white killer whale floated several meters from their boat, its huge eye watching them.

It dived and then came arcing up out of the water before going under again, this time sinking like a submarine. They'd seen killer whales in the fjords before, but never so close up.

"Marit—right! Go right!"

"Whose right?" Uncertain, she pulled to her right and Lars screamed.

"No, not that way!"

She pulled hard on her left oar.

In the next second, on her left, a bobbing round metal object paralleled them, floating beyond the tip of Marit's oar.

*A mine.*

She eased both oars out of the water and brought them in closer to the gunwales. Bestefar had said that if you so much as brushed into a mine, it could explode. She froze, waiting as the distance grew between the floating mine and their little boat, centimeter by slow centimeter.

When they were clear of the mine, Marit rowed again, leaving it farther and farther in their wake. She felt sick about what might have happened. She glanced over her shoulder to Lars, perched on the bow. "You saved us," she called, her voice tremulous. *"Takk."*

He nodded but didn't turn from his duty.

Waves pushed them closer toward Giske Island. Ahead, a church steeple pierced the heavy sky. "See that church?" She tried to sound calmer than she felt.

"*Ja.*"

"Mama and Papa told me it's a few hundred years old, but the smaller chapel is even older. It was built by a powerful Viking family a thousand years ago."

"Really?"

"I'd swear on the Bible." This time, she was telling the truth. She tried to imagine people living on these remote islands so many years ago. Somehow thinking about them gave her hope. The Nazis seemed to have taken over her whole world, but even they couldn't stay in power forever.

Sooner than expected, their boat slammed forward, jolting them off their seats. She fell backward onto the wet floor of the boat, banging her shoulder. When she scrambled to her feet to look around, Lars had disappeared.

Marit scrambled over the bow of the rowboat. On the sandy shore, face down, lay her brother.

"Lars! Are you all right?"

He sat up slowly and brushed wet sand off his skinned nose. His lower lip quivered. "I'm cold."

"Then we'll find someplace to get warm." The white beach merged with gray pastures. Clusters of sheep stared at them, round and fat in their dirty white coats. "Let's try the church."

They pulled the rowboat onto the sandy shore. There

was nowhere to tie it, so they left it there. Then they ran across the pasture to the red-roofed stone church beyond. Unlike Norway's many octagonal churches, this one was rectangular, with a two-sided pitched roof; it was surrounded by a thick stone fence, which ended in two stone pillars. They passed through, hand in hand.

Ahead, a red and black Nazi flag hung above the door. Marit stopped, reluctant to move any closer.

But they needed shelter. Gusts of wind turned to torrents of rain. Her teeth chattered with cold. Lars's skin had gone from greenish gray to gray-blue. He needed to get out of the foul weather, to be dry and warm. Maybe they'd be lucky. Maybe the church was empty. They would stop for a short time, then hope for the winds to change so they could row back.

"Come on." She darted to the heavy wooden door, knocked, waited a full ten seconds . . . and then stepped in. Straight, ornately carved pews waited beneath the carved pulpit, off to the left.

Marit motioned to Lars to sit down beside her in the back of the church. She pulled off her slicker and hung it on the back of the pew. It was cold in the church, but warm compared to the wet, howling winds beyond its walls.

Her arms were heavy anchors. If she curled up in a ball and let her clothes dry out, and slept . . . just a short nap . . . She closed her eyes. She'd never felt so tired before. Rain pounded on the roof, pelted the paned windows, and created a sense of coziness, even though the building was cool.

Lars stirred in the pew beside her, but she gave in to exhaustion and slept.

## CHAPTER TWENTY-ONE

# Troubled Mission

Marit awoke to the deep voices of men. She was in a church, she remembered quickly, but why?

"A sister?" said a man in a melodic voice. Then it all flooded back. Rowing to the fishing village, asking for klipfish and leaving the compass in the hands of a strange man, and then getting swept by southwesterly winds to Giske Island. "Where? Show us."

Footsteps approached. It must be a pastor, someone who would help them. Expectantly and with a sense of relief, Marit opened her eyes. Lars stood at the edge of her pew, pointing. Behind him glowered the faces of two men: a Nazi soldier and an officer.

Marit jumped to the worst conclusions: They'd been found out, caught as part of the Resistance. But she tried to hide her fears. She rubbed her eyes, faked a wide yawn, and blinked.

The officer said something in German, and the soldier interpreted it in Norwegian. "What are you kids doing here?"

Lars's chin began to quiver.

*No, Lars . . . not now!* Marit thought. *Please don't tell about our trip.*

She debated if she should remain silent, as always, but decided to risk speaking. "School's closed," she started and cleared her throat.

Lars began to whimper, and his whimpers turned to crying.

Marit talked faster, hoping her brother would hold his tongue. "We were bored," she continued, "so we went rowing this morning and the wind was so strong it blew us off course." She pointed to the weather outside the windows and told him that they came from Godøy. "I couldn't row back, so we came into the church for shelter. I hope we didn't break any rules. We weren't trying to be trouble for anyone. We don't want to be a problem."

She surprised herself at how easily the words rolled off her tongue. She had never been good at lying. The war was apparently changing that.

The soldier related her story to the officer, and then asked, "What is your name?"

"Marit Gundersen. And this is my brother, Lars."

The soldier raised his voice above Lars's snuffles. "The enemy may try to attack on this coast and we want to keep you safe. You seem like smart kids. Tell us, have you seen anything on your island that seems unusual?"

"*Nei.*"

"Think harder. Anything out of the ordinary—visitors, perhaps? Faces you haven't seen before. Five men, perhaps, wearing oilskins and sea boots? Anyone with anything to hide? Anything unusual?"

She tilted her head, as if seriously considering his questions. She pictured Henrik's oilskin boots, one in shreds around his badly injured foot. He had said his boat had gone down. Had the other four all died? This question about anything *unusual* was almost laughable.

With a casual shrug of her shoulders, she replied with amazing outward calm. "*Nei.*" For extra effect, as if she were genuinely trying to think hard, she paused. Then, hoping to persuade Lars to not add a word, she slowly shook her head at him, then at the soldier. "Nothing unusual."

She hoped she'd convinced him.

He spoke again in German with the officer, then turned to her, his face revealing nothing. "Gather your things," he ordered, "and come with me."

In the pouring rain, Marit and Lars followed the soldier to the nearest house. He knocked—*bam, bam, bam, bam.* Behind them in the distance, in the shelter of the church doorway, the officer smoked a cigarette.

The tallest woman Marit had ever met opened the door. To her chest she held a crying infant. *"Ja?"*

"By orders of the Reich, give these children shelter and return them to Godøy where they belong."

"Return them? But my husband—"

The soldier snapped his arm straight toward her head. *"Heil Hitler!"* he shouted, then walked away.

The woman stood board stiff. Her baby bawled harder. Then she turned her attention to Marit and Lars, as if seeing them for the first time. Her shoulders relaxed and she exhaled. *"Vel,"* she said. "You'd better come inside. It's a foul day." Once the door was closed and locked, she added with scorn, "But for the Nazis, compared to the hell that awaits *their* souls, this weather will someday seem like heaven."

Marit smiled. She liked this woman.

"My husband is fishing, and you'll have to stay here until he returns. I have no way to get you back to Godøy before then."

A small fire crackled in the cookstove. As she placed her baby in a basket on the counter, she motioned with her head to a bench at the table. "Sit," she said, "and hand me your wet clothes." They removed their layers, right down to their thin wool undergarments, and she hung their clothes on a line that stretched from one end of the kitchen to the other. Bright yellow dishes decorated the open shelves. A red runner graced the simple wooden table. Marit enjoyed the comfort of being in this home. She thought of the many times she'd sat at her own kitchen table in Isfjorden with Papa and Mama. The scents of fresh coffee, wood smoke, and homemade flatbread, fresh from the oven. She'd give almost anything to go back to those times.

The woman added a birch log to the cookstove, and before long, heat billowed, warming them and drying their clothes. She poured mugs of hot water. "Something to warm you," she said. Arms across her chest, she studied them, then turned to her nearly bare cupboards and icebox. Soon, she laid out a few pieces of pickled herring and two pieces of bread.

"*Takk,*" Marit said, knowing that with food increasingly scarce, this was a generous gift, a banquet. She and Lars huddled side by side and ate hungrily.

They soon learned that the woman's name was Johanne, and that she was originally from Bergen on the mainland. "With this war, I'm beginning to wonder if anything is left standing there anymore." The Allies, she said, had hit several German targets, including ships.

"And the Germans bomb any building that they think is connected with Resistance activities. The world has turned upside down."

What would Johanne think if Marit told her she was helping the Resistance and hiding a soldier? She had an impulse to tell this woman everything, but she held back. Because of her actions, she must be extra careful to guard her secrets so no harm would come to Johanne's family.

Johanne told them a joke. "A knock came at the door," she began, "and the old woman asked, 'Who is it?'

"'The Angel of Death,' came the reply. The woman opened the door and smiled. 'Come in, come in! I thought you were the Gestapo!'"

Marit laughed, but Lars scrunched his forehead in confusion.

"The Angel of Death," Johanne explained, "even *that* looks good compared to the Gestapo—the Nazis' secret police. Get it?"

He nodded. "I knew that."

Johanne told them how when the radios were recently turned in on Giske Island, the villagers put their radios on a horse-drawn cart, draped it in black, and followed the cart like a funeral procession. "We even sang hymns," she said, "accompanied by fiddle."

Marit told Johanne about the bombing of their real home at Isfjorden, about staying with Bestefar on Godøy

Island, and about Aunt Ingeborg being taken away in the middle of the school day.

"Oh, dear." Johanne's shoulders rose slowly. She looked at them with sympathy. "And your parents, are they alive?"

"They've sent letters," Lars said.

"Good," Johanne said. "That's good. With this war, you never know."

What Johanne said was true. Marit's parents could be killed any day—any second—by air attacks, or found out by the Gestapo. But her parents were still in the mountains, Marit tried to console herself, tucked safely away from harm. At least, that was her prayer.

"My husband won't be back until later. Read or rest, whatever you like. He'll get you home. Not that I like the idea of his crossing the waters at night, mind you, but we've been given no choice, have we?"

"*Nei,*" Marit replied.

The baby started to fuss, and Johanne moved to a corner rocker to nurse.

From a shelf, Marit pulled down a book called *Kristin Lavransdatter: The Bridal Wreath.* She opened the novel and began reading aloud about a Norwegian girl in the Middle Ages and her struggle to survive in difficult times. Marit knew Lars loved to be read to. And she had loved it when Mama had read to them every night.

That afternoon in the living room, sitting shoulder to

shoulder with Lars on the braided wool rug, Marit read until her voice grew hoarse. Before long, Lars stretched out his legs, lay his head down, and fell asleep. And still Marit read, partly because Lars's body, snuggled against hers, was comforting. And partly because she couldn't put the book down. It took her away from the present and everything her world had become. It silenced her concerns about returning to Godøy. It helped her pretend they could stay here with Johanne instead. What would Bestefar do when he learned of their misadventure? And the soldier in the loft. What if Bestefar found him? Would he stay quiet and hidden while she was away? It was easier to keep turning the page of the book than to answer such questions.

By late afternoon, to their fortune, the wind and rain had eased. When Lars stirred, Marit put the book back, went to the kitchen, and talked with Johanne. "The wind seems to have died down. I think I could row back."

"It's too far, and it's growing dark."

"But I'm a strong rower," she said, her arms and shoulders aching.

Johanne shook her head. "That may be, but you were put in my charge, and I'm not going to let another wind toss you back up on our shore. For your sake and for mine. The less often those Nazis come to my door, the better. You'll stay and wait until Rollo returns. He'll motor you back."

Marit didn't have to wait long. Within the hour, Johanne's husband returned, and then wordlessly he bade them to follow. In the thickening darkness, he towed their empty rowboat behind his trawler.

At considerable risk, they slowly crossed the water between the two islands and rounded the peninsula of the familiar lighthouse. Marit was told to watch for mines, but how was she to see them in such dark waters?

Suddenly, a shot rang out and water sprayed before the bow. She screamed.

From the lighthouse, rays of light swept across the boat.

*"Halt!"*

Rollo idled the motor. "These children," Rollo shouted, "drifted in their rowboat to Giske! We were ordered to return them here, where they live!"

There was no answer, just lights washing back and forth over the deck, illuminating them. Water lapped against the boat and rocked them from side to side.

Marit held on to the boat's mast with Lars. "Just stay calm," she whispered, "don't talk."

"Proceed!" the soldier shouted.

Rollo shifted from neutral to forward, and they made their way slowly from the lighthouse to the wharf. In the distance, shadowy shapes looked increasingly familiar.

"There's the pier," Marit called. "Up ahead."

Without a word, Rollo eased the boat slowly into the

harbor and pulled up beside an open dock. "Stay home," he said, almost the only words he'd said the whole way. "You put others in danger."

"*Takk,*" Marit said.

He motioned to their rowboat tied to the stern of his trawler. She and Lars hopped down into it as he untied it from his boat and pushed it away.

Marit picked up the oars and rowed the short distance to the dark silhouette of Bestefar's boathouse. As she pulled through the black water, her shoulder muscles, back, and hands protested in pain. She was more sore than she'd ever been in her life.

They touched shore, hopped out, and pulled up the rowboat. Marit almost wanted to kiss the stones beneath her feet. They had made it back. They were safe! As they passed the boathouse's side door, it creaked open.

They jumped, and Lars seized Marit's arm.

"Marit!" Bestefar spoke harshly.

She took in the figure darkening the door frame. He would never forgive her for being gone so long with the rowboat, no matter what excuse she tried to come up with now. He'd spoken one word, and by his tone, she understood clearly where he was placing the blame.

## CHAPTER TWENTY-TWO

# Infection

"Straight home!" Bestefar ordered. Without another word, he marched them down the road. Marit glanced at the barn as they passed. She needed to check on Henrik, to bring him food and water and tell him that she'd delivered the compass. All that would have to wait until Bestefar went to bed.

In the warmth of the kitchen, Bestefar paced, his eyebrows meeting in a white, furrowed *V*.

"It wasn't Lars's idea to row out so far, that much I know. Marit, I think it's best you go to bed early tonight."

"But I'm starving!"

"You'll survive until morning. No, your punishment is

to head straight upstairs. You've caused me enough worry. You need to ponder your foolishness."

Marit drank a cup of water from the hand pump at the sink, and then paused at the first step, wondering about Henrik. He needed food. He needed water. Perhaps if Marit told Bestefar the truth, he'd help her care for him. Maybe call a doctor. But she came to a quick decision—the same one she'd come to earlier. To tell Bestefar was to risk Henrik's life further.

"Marit!"

Her anger toward Bestefar burned all the hotter as she stomped loudly up the stairs.

"That's enough for one day," Bestefar called after her. "Not another word, not another foot stomping, do you understand?"

She refused to answer.

Stretched out on her bed, she listened to her stomach rumble with hunger. She'd never felt more tired. Every muscle in her body was filled with lead. And she was really, really hungry. But she would not beg. She was too proud to plead for something to eat. Still, it wasn't fair that Lars was allowed to eat a bowl of cod stew. Far from the wood stove, her bedroom was cool; Aunt Ingeborg's homemade wool socks and her own sweaters barely warmed her.

Even Lars made her angry. His voice flitted up the stairs, chatting on and on to Bestefar about being on the water and the wind blowing them straight to Giske and spotting a killer whale. "And we nearly bumped into a floating mine," he added, "but I told Marit to turn right."

She held her breath and waited for him to tell every bit of their day and get her in real trouble.

"But she turned fast," he said, "and we missed it completely!"

To her relief, Lars didn't mention anything about the fishing village or the church on Giske or the Germans. "A nice woman named Johanne gave us food and I fell asleep."

From what she could hear, Lars was intentionally steering clear of telling everything. "We're safe and that's what matters," he said, sounding just like Papa.

Bestefar humphed. "We're in the middle of a war," he said, seeming to talk more to himself than to Lars. "I have enough to worry about without my grandchildren wandering off—across open water, no less."

Her mind replayed her long day. What had the German soldier on Giske Island meant when he said "The enemy may try to attack on this coast"? Did that mean the Allied forces were planning to land somewhere on Norway's western coast? She wondered if delivering the compass was part of such a plan. Did it carry codes in the engravings or, somewhere inside its case, a small note of importance? Had anyone seen her on the doorstep of the house in Alnes?

Before she knew it, she had dropped into a fathomless sleep.

Lars's moaning and leg-kicking woke her. He was sound asleep, and she was grateful that she no longer had to wake him to use the night pot. From the main floor, Bestefar's snoring whistled through the house—a good sign.

She slipped into her boots, *jakke,* and hat. Then, silent as a mole, she grabbed a half loaf of something that passed for bread—as Aunt Ingeborg had said, the flour was more like ground sand these days. She broke off a chunk of cheese from the wheel in the icebox. She poured a glass of milk, ate quickly, then stuffed Henrik's half of the cheese and bread in her pockets. This time, Big Olga would have to wait.

Climbing the ladder to the loft with a half bucketful of water, Marit was met with air so foul she nearly tumbled backward.

"Henrik?" she whispered, then clasped her hand over her nose.

She should have left him an empty bucket to use, but that hadn't occurred to her. He was in no shape to climb up and down the ladder. He surely couldn't have hiked to the outhouse. She was a foolish child taking on tasks far larger than she could possibly handle.

If the Gestapo returned to the farm to search again—and especially if they brought search dogs with them—

the smell in the loft would flash a signal brighter than any lighthouse. She knelt beside the soldier.

"Henrik?" No answer.

He was dead—there could be no other explanation. Panic built in her legs. She wanted to run away but forced herself to stay calm. She reached into the pile of straw and touched his chest. Beneath her palm, she sensed breathing—breaths as shallow as a parched riverbed.

Marit brushed straw from his face. His eyes were sunken behind shadowed lids. A white crusty film covered his cracked lips. She touched his forehead. He was burning with fever.

"*Mor,*" he cried weakly, like a child calling out for his mother.

"Oh—you are alive!" She brushed more straw from his body. Careful not to bump him, she examined his injured foot. It was swollen to three times its earlier size, and the open wounds oozed. She didn't know much about medicine, but she knew that his foot was dangerously infected. His fever was possibly high enough to kill him.

She lifted a ladle of water to his lips, but it dripped across his face. Some of it fell into his parted lips. She tried to give him more, and he opened his mouth wider but choked, spitting water, which dribbled down his neck. If he was too weak to drink . . .

"Don't die on me, Henrik," she whispered. "I delivered

it—the compass—just like you asked." She didn't know if he could hear her or, if he did, whether he understood.

The sky was growing hazy with a dusky morning light. Bestefar could be leaving for his boat at any moment, and Marit needed to be milking Big Olga when he stepped from the farmhouse, just in case he checked on her. She gently placed more fresh straw over Henrik, hoping to hide the foul odor, and then headed down the ladder. "I'll get help, I promise."

From her stanchion, Big Olga studied Marit as she skillfully eased the cow's full udders with her hands. The barn cat and her kittens showed up, right on schedule, and waited for their taste of warm morning milk. Before foamy milk had covered the base of the bucket, the barn door opened.

"Marit?" Bestefar stepped in.

She didn't answer, even though she knew it was rude not to do so. She was afraid that if she said a word, her true feelings—about him, about his unwillingness to take action, about brave Henrik lying overhead, whose life was quickly unwinding like a skein of yarn—would all come out of her mouth and she would say too much. She bit the soft, fleshy inside of her lips.

*"God morgen,"* he said, his voice softer than the night before. She sensed him moving closer, standing behind her as she leaned over the bucket, sheltered by the steady

breathing of Big Olga. Marit tensed, hoping that he wouldn't notice the smell from the loft.

"Marit, it's not that I don't—" he began, then stopped. "I was terribly worried last night when you two were not at dinner. And then the rowboat was gone."

She kept milking—*ting, ting, ting*—aiming the white stream against the side of the can. Though he was apologizing in his own way, and she felt she should at least acknowledge him, she held herself in check. She wasn't ready to let go of her anger.

From the corner of her eye she watched him. He slid his hands into his trouser pockets and filled his lungs with one deep, long breath. When she didn't turn or say anything, he exhaled in a huff, stepped away, and headed out through the barn door, most likely to his boat.

With hands trembling from anger and fright, Marit continued milking. To her relief, the smell from the loft hadn't sent him up the ladder to investigate.

After turning Big Olga out to pasture, Marit knew what she had to do.

"Lars," she said, calling into the house. "Wait here. I'll be back soon!"

Then she dashed down the road, cutting over paths from the general store to Hanna's home, a red clapboard with a porch overlooking the water. Marit banged on the door, trying to catch her breath, and waited.

"Marit!" Hanna said, still in her pajamas. "It's early, but come in. I've missed you, with school out."

Marit stayed on the porch and shook her head.

Hanna's cheerful expression faded. "What happened? Marit, are you OK?" She glanced across the water toward Ålesund. "Oh, no. Did you get bad news about your parents?"

"I need your mother," Marit said.

"She's still at the hospital in Ålesund. The war keeps her busy. She should return in an hour on the first boat. Why?"

Marit didn't know what to do. She had nowhere else to turn. "He made me promise not to tell anyone about him. But if he doesn't get help, he's going to die."

"Who?"

She couldn't return alone. Not without a plan, without help. In a whisper, she told Hanna about the soldier hidden in the loft. "You must not say a word about this. Not to anyone, Hanna."

"I promise."

Marit waited for Mrs. Brottem at the wharf, and when the mail boat chugged into the harbor, she looked for a red scarf and navy wool coat, just as Hanna had described. Since Marit had seen her last, Mrs. Brottem had gathered deep lines across her forehead.

As passengers stepped from the boat, Marit stopped her. "Mrs. Brottem?"

"Why, Marit," she said, a tired smile turning to concern. "Is everything all right with Hanna and my babies?"

"They're fine," Marit said. "It's my brother, Lars." She lied. "Could you please come check on him? He's in a bad way with a fever."

"Of course."

## CHAPTER TWENTY-THREE

# Warning

With Mrs. Brottem walking alongside, Marit headed toward the barn. Lars was outside, petting the gray goat.

"Your brother certainly seems fine now," Mrs. Brottem said, pausing on the dirt drive.

"It's not really Lars," Marit said in a rush. "I'm sorry. I had to say that because of the other passengers. Please. I'll show you. In the barn."

"I don't know anything about farm animals, Marit."

"Lars," Marit said, pushing open the barn door. "Keep watch and let us know if anyone is coming. Can you do that?"

"*Ja,*" he said. "I'm good at that."

For the next hour, Marit assisted Mrs. Brottem, supplying her with buckets of warm water. Tucking her strawberry blond hair back into her scarf and washing her hands, Mrs. Brottem set to work. She didn't fret and she didn't smile, but she held the edge of her lower lip between her teeth as she examined the soldier.

She cut the pants right off the soldier's legs. "Don't worry," she told Henrik, who slipped in and out of consciousness. "I promise to sew them back up after they get a good washing."

Marit took his clothes down to where a wash bucket waited, then scrubbed and cleaned his torn and soiled pants. When she returned, wet cloths covered Henrik's forehead and Mrs. Brottem ladled water into his mouth, sometimes smoothing his throat with her fingers to help him swallow.

"It's your foot that's causing all this trouble," she told him. "It's badly infected. I'm going to use some hot compresses, and it will hurt, but you must be quiet. Marit, hand me a clean rag."

Marit handed her one from the pile she'd gathered.

Mrs. Brottem put the cloth in the soldier's mouth. "Bite on this if you must."

Then, she faced the twisted and raw stump of his foot and shook her head. "We should get a doctor here to you, but there isn't one on the island. Marit, your grandfather will have to ferry one over from Ålesund—and they're very busy there, too."

"*Nei.* We can't tell Bestefar!" Marit pleaded.

"Why not? This soldier needs help."

Ashamed of her grandfather, Marit felt heat rise to her face. "I'm worried he'll report Henrik to the Nazis."

Finally, Mrs. Brottem spoke. "Oh. I see." She examined the soldier's foot further. "I'll see what I can do first, but if his foot must be amputated, then we'll have to risk telling him."

Eyes tight with pain, Henrik bit down on the cloth and moaned as Mrs. Brottem swabbed his infected foot. Marit couldn't stand to see anyone in such pain and looked away. But it was either pain or certain death.

"Let's hope that by cleaning the infected wounds he'll take a turn for the better. I'll return tomorrow morning before heading across to the hospital. You must make sure he drinks plenty of water so he doesn't get dehydrated. And if he's warm, use a cold, wet cloth to keep the fever down. When I return, if he's not better, I will speak with your grandfather myself."

Marit nodded.

As Mrs. Brottem lingered to stitch up the other pant leg as Marit watched Henrik. His eyes were a little brighter, his breathing deeper.

His gaze met Marit's, and she guessed his question. "Did you . . ." he began.

She nodded with a smile. "*Ja.* Just as you asked. It's done."

*"Tusen takk,"* he said. "I owe you a great debt."

Mrs. Brottem must have thought he was speaking to her, for she answered, "Marit—she did the most. But don't thank us yet," she said, her voice stern. "You're not well yet. *Rest.* And do your best to use this pot when you must."

Later, as they headed down the loft ladder, Mrs. Brottem whispered, "This war. None of us can handle it alone. But this boy . . . Henrik . . . without the risks you took to save him, Marit, he'd be dead by now. He owes *you* his life. You've been very brave."

They stood by the cow stanchion as Lars continued his lookout.

*"Nei."* Marit shook her head back and forth. "I've been terrified, scared to death that—"

"Marit," Hanna's mother interrupted. "You didn't let your fears stop you from . . . doing what needed to be done. *That's* bravery."

That afternoon, Henrik's fever dropped, and he drank water greedily from the ladle Marit held to his lips. He managed a bowl of thin cod stew, which Marit fed him spoonful by slow spoonful. Then he dropped back, exhausted.

At supper, Lars carried on with Bestefar as if the day

had been just like any other. He talked about missing school, how cold he was at night now without the *dyne,* and about becoming a fisherman someday. Marit was glad for his chatter. She could stay tucked within her silence. She wouldn't have to try to lie about her day.

A knock—so light that she wondered if she'd imagined it—sounded at the door. She dropped her spoon against the edge of her bowl, and cod stew splattered across the table. What if Henrik had managed to climb down the ladder? Maybe he was feverish again—possibly delirious. She had warned him about Bestefar, and that it wasn't safe to come to the house.

Or worse, the Gestapo had returned to do another search. Worse than the Angel of Death. Marit remained statue-still.

Bestefar was at the door, easing it open, clearing his throat. Marit stared at her nearly empty bowl and listened. Whatever bravery she might have shown earlier was no longer in her grasp. She was certain of that.

"Mr. Halversen, my name is Olaf," the voice came. "Olaf Andersen."

Marit jerked her gaze toward the door.

"I need to talk to you."

On the doorstep stood Olaf, with Kaptain at his side, his tail curved over his back. Olaf removed his cap, ran one hand through his untamable hair, and turned his cap round and round between both hands. Why was he here? It made no sense. And to be out after dark was to risk getting stopped by the Gestapo. But his parents were NS—traitors. Maybe that's why he was free to roam about despite the curfew.

"I came to warn you," he said, looking beyond Bestefar to Marit. "I heard my parents talking with a German officer. I . . . I hear more than I should. But I came to tell you that there will be a crackdown on the island. 'A severe crackdown,' the German said. I thought you should know."

A surge of fear zinged through her body. Was it possible that Olaf knew about her helping the Resistance soldier? Did he know about her having delivered the compass? But how could he? He had always acted as if he wanted to be friends. Had he been spying on her all along?

Bestefar said quietly, "They've searched here already! What more do we have to worry about? Maybe you're trying to trap us." He stepped closer to Olaf, towering over him.

Olaf glanced questioningly from Marit to Bestefar, then took a step back.

"Go," Bestefar said icily, his hand clamped on the edge of the door, ready to close on Olaf's shoes. "Now."

Olaf yanked on his cap and backed down the steps. "I . . . I'm only trying to help."

"Bestefar," Marit pleaded. She suddenly felt sorry for

Olaf. If he was forced away so soon, they would never know more about his warning or what he actually *knew* about her efforts to help Henrik. "Wait, um, shouldn't we hear him out?"

"*Nei.*"

Before Bestefar had closed the door, Marit slipped outside and flew down the steps after Olaf. "Wait!"

The damp ground soaked through her wool socks. Beyond the barn, a crescent moon hung low in the night sky. She made out the shadowy figures of Olaf and his dog as they headed toward the road.

"Olaf, wait!"

He stopped and slowly turned. Then he walked back, his face mostly in shadow, lit only by a hint of moonlight reflecting off patches of melting snow. Kaptain sat down immediately at his side.

"I'm sorry," she said, tilting her head toward the farmhouse, "for what happened in there. Thank you for warning us, even if I don't understand."

"Your grandfather doesn't want to hear the truth, does he?"

"He wants peace," she said. "He thinks if he avoids trouble—" She stopped. She had no excuses for Bestefar.

The night air was icy with mist. Marit wrapped her arms around herself. Her breath hovered in tiny clouds. "At school," she started, not sure exactly what she was going to say, "I'm sorry I never talked with you. I hope you understand. I can't. It's not you. I don't believe you're one of them."

"Them?" He sounded bitter. "Who, my parents?"

"*Nei*, I mean . . . NS . . . you're not a Nazi."

"Marit," he said. "You don't even *know* me."

She thought of the day he'd carried Kaptain, just a puppy, from the wharf—so proud, so excited. His father had brought back a puppy for Olaf when most people were worrying about the cost of eggs. She didn't know everything about Olaf's parents, and she didn't know everything about Olaf, but she knew him well enough. "I know you're good, Olaf. And I know I'm sorry for so much. You tried to warn us. What can I do?"

"Just believe me." His voice softened to a plea. "I've heard talk. When one family member is taken away, the others look more suspicious. I'm worried you might be at risk."

The door opened and Bestefar stood in the doorway. He cleared his throat. Before he ordered her to come inside, Marit said quickly, "It's the war, Olaf. Maybe someday things will be different."

"Maybe," Olaf said. Then he turned his back and hurried away, absorbed into the damp night.

## CHAPTER TWENTY-FOUR

# At Risk

Marit couldn't sleep. Bestefar's snoring rose through the floor vents like the snorting of a hibernating bear. As much as Marit tried to stay angry with him for the brusque way he had treated Olaf, her own conversation with Olaf bothered her more.

"Your family is at risk," Olaf had said. In her heart, she believed Olaf was good, but how could she know for sure? How long could anyone be "iced out" before they turned bitter and angry? He *had* risked much by coming to warn them of a crackdown. But was Bestefar right? Was it possible that Olaf had sided with the NS and was warning them as a ploy, a way of getting them to confide in him and to reveal something secret? Or had he come to warn them as a friend would? What exactly had he overheard? In a world where all the rules had changed, she couldn't know anything for sure.

Just as she learned by listening to the sounds around her, and paying attention, she would listen with her heart. And her heart told her that Olaf had meant only good.

She drifted in and out of sleep. Sometime later, she awoke. Outside, a storm was gathering. Waves rushed the shore beyond the farmhouse. Sleet pelted the windowpanes. Wind taunted the farmhouse, and overhead slate shingles trembled.

Footsteps sounded up the stairs.

"Marit?" came Bestefar's deep voice. "Lars?"

Bundled like a bear in foul-weather clothing, he ordered, "Get up. Put on your warm clothes. Hurry now and come with me."

"Is your boat loose?" Marit asked. A thousand possibilities came to her. He'd found the soldier in the loft. The Gestapo were here, beginning their crackdown. Maybe there was a fire. Bombing—it had started again. She sat up, trying to get her bearings. She didn't feel like getting out of bed if she didn't have to. It was the middle of the night and the air was icy. "But why?"

"Just follow. Do as I say. And for God's sake, hurry." Then he headed down the stairs.

She thought of the morning when bombs first fell and

Mama and Papa insisted they go downstairs. Like then, this wasn't a time to delay. "Wake up," she said, shaking Lars's shoulder. "Bestefar said we have to get up and follow him." He moaned.

Marit pushed him to a sitting position, swung his legs over the side of the bed, and helped him to his feet. They didn't have to worry much about adding warm clothes, since they were already dressed in nearly everything they owned. They made their way downstairs and found their boots beside the door. She helped Lars, who was more asleep than awake.

For a moment, they waited at the door, ready to go. Lars leaned into her.

"Bestefar," Marit said, sure he'd discovered their soldier for sure. "Just tell us—"

"I'll tell you soon enough," he said. "But Marit, just this once," he said, his voice full of pleading. "Don't argue with me!"

Moments later they were following him out the door. "Not a word," he said, his hand raised up to them as they crossed from the house toward the barn. Marit braced herself for questions about Henrik. But he walked right past the barn without a glance. Instead, he hurried through sleet, rain, and wind to the road. In a night as dense as peat, they could easily lose him. Marit grabbed Lars's hand and scurried to keep up. Freezing rain lashed her face. Never had she seen Bestefar move so fast. He was nearly running.

Then, in her stomach, the reason for this strange leave-taking struck. Olaf's warning. This had something to do with his visit. But what?

Her whole body tensed, filled with questions and apprehension. They had no excuse for being out in the middle of the night. If a Nazi soldier stopped them, they would all be in terrible trouble. They could be shot on sight.

They skirted the ditches on the way to the boathouse. Bestefar paused, waiting for them to catch up. Then he pulled them into a huddle so that their heads touched. "Not a word," he whispered. "Not a sound until we're inside. Do you understand?"

They nodded. With the Nazi headquarters in the schoolhouse just down the road, Marit wasn't about to protest. Still, this whole thing was crazy. Maybe that was it. Bestefar truly had gone crazy.

Ahead, the boathouse beckoned like a fortress. They followed him through the side door. One step, two. She stopped, waiting. Surely he'd light a candle or help them see somehow. There was a scratch and the smell of sulfur, then the flicker of a candle glowed in Bestefar's hand. And there, coming toward her from a cluster of huddled shapes in the corner, shedding a blanket as she drew closer, was a face that sent Marit's heart on wings.

Aunt Ingeborg!

Marit wanted to cry out loud, to scream with joy. She expected the vision would vanish like a dream, but Aunt Ingeborg, dressed in oversize men's clothing, drew her and Lars into a tight hug, the scratchy wool of her *jakke* against Marit's face. This was no dream.

"Oh, Marit! Lars!" Aunt Ingeborg whispered.

"How did you get here?" Marit asked, her voice hushed. "I saw them haul you away! I thought I'd never see you again." A hundred questions tumbled within her.

"Our German truck was ambushed—soon after we left Ålesund. Three of us teachers were in hiding, until yesterday. Our guide received a signal—brought us here to wait for the next bus."

"What bus?" she whispered. There were no buses on the island.

"Not a real bus," Bestefar interjected. "We'll go from here to Scotland's Shetland Islands. The fishing boats that ferry back and forth—we call them 'The Shetland Bus.'"

## CHAPTER TWENTY-FIVE

# Valuable Cargo

"Everyone, listen!" Bestefar said, his voice commanding, even at a whisper. He spoke not only to them but also to five people in the shadows. In the ring of the candle's faint light, Marit noticed three men (one with a dark beard, one with a rifle slung across his shoulder, another with a bandage over both eyes) and two women (one whose cape stretched across her protruding belly, the other older, in a calf-length coat). Marit could not understand why Bestefar seemed to be in the middle of this. And how could he know of this plan to take "The Shetland Bus"?

"You will hide quietly in the hold, shoulder to shoulder, tight as sardines," he began.

Not only could Marit barely see, but she struggled to grasp the meaning of what she was hearing.

"Me, too?" Lars asked with excitement. Aunt Ingeborg pulled him close. "*Shhhh.*"

Marit was completely stunned. The man she had turned her anger toward, whom she had accused of being as spineless as a boiled potato, was part of the Resistance?

"You won't be comfortable," he explained to everyone, "but whatever happens on deck, you must all remain below—and absolutely silent. Am I clear?"

Marit tried to catch up with all that was coming to light.

"There's no time to waste. Let's board the bus," he said. "We'll ferry out in the dinghy to the trawler."

The Shetland Islands were over three hundred kilometers away. It was stormy, the worst kind of weather and the wrong season to make that kind of voyage.

Marit's mind buzzed with questions, but this wasn't the time to ask them. She understood the risk of making any more noise than necessary. But what about Mama and Papa? Was she to leave Norway and leave them behind? Then she remembered. She grabbed Bestefar's sleeve.

"There's a soldier—a Resistance soldier—in the barn loft. He's wounded. I've been hiding him. If we don't go back for him, the Gestapo will find him."

"In the loft? *Our* loft?" Bestefar said. His silence was filled with foreboding. "If we go back for anyone now, we risk the whole mission."

"And if we don't, he'll die. We can't leave him!" Marit headed toward the door. "I'm the one who told him to hide there. I'll go."

Bestefar glanced around, as if weighing the value of his cargo. "Not alone," he said. "It's better if I join you. We must hurry. The rest of you—row out and take your places in the boat's hold. Ingeborg, guide them. We'll return quickly, God willing. If anything should happen to us, get word to Einar. He'll know what to do." Einar, Marit knew, was another local fisherman—apparently working, too, for the Resistance.

Marit forced herself to leave Aunt Ingeborg and Lars. She had to help Henrik.

Heads tucked, she and Bestefar braved the pelting sleet.

"Shouldn't we stay in the ditches?" she whispered.

He shook his head. "They're accustomed to seeing me at this hour. If we're stopped, let me do the talking."

No sooner had they rounded the first bend than lights bore down on them from behind. Marit scuttled out of the way, but not before a truck splashed past her, then squealed its brakes to a stop. She and Bestefar continued walking until they were alongside the vehicle. Its window opened, and a flashlight blinded them.

Marit covered her eyes with her mitten, hoping to keep from giving away her dread.

"What are you doing out past curfew?"

"I'm sorry, sir," Bestefar said. "I had to check on my fishing boat. The bilge pump has not been working, and I had to make sure she wasn't taking on water."

The light fell squarely on Marit. "And you?"

"She's my granddaughter."

"*Nei!*" the soldier shouted, and with a swift motion through the open window, hit Bestefar across his face with a pistol.

Bestefar stumbled back. Marit gasped, but held herself still.

"She must answer for herself," barked the soldier.

If she didn't speak up this time, Marit was certain the soldier would hurt Bestefar far worse than he already had.

"The night is so awful," she said, "I didn't want Bestefar to be out all alone. He didn't want me to come, but I followed him."

The soldier humphed. "To have such devotion, old man. You're lucky."

"*Ja,*" Bestefar said. "Marit is my pride and joy."

Despite the bleak situation, she tucked away his words.

"Get home quick, before your luck runs out." Then the Nazi soldier motioned to the driver, and the wheels churned forward, kicking up a spray of freezing water. The wind whined and churned up the sea so that it roared against the shore below. Marit and Bestefar pressed home, nearly at a run, without a word. Some encounters were too close to even speak about.

The barn and farmhouse sat dark and lonely. Marit opened the barn door, and Bestefar followed her inside. She clambered up the loft ladder. "Henrik! We must get you out of here."

The loft was silent.

"Henrik?"

She fumbled in the darkness and found him. She removed her mittens and reached out to touch his face. The moment her hands touched his nose and forehead, she gasped. His skin was stiff and cold. Lifeless. She leaned forward and touched her head to his chest, hoping for the sound of a faint heartbeat, the slightest breath of air. But she was too late. Her efforts to save him had not been nearly enough.

She had failed him.

She eased his stiff eyelids shut with her fingertips. Though her throat ached, she whispered, *"God natt."* Good night.

Then she nearly stumbled down the ladder, her chest shuddering.

"Marit," Bestefar said, catching her.

The low moan of a wounded animal rose from her

core. Her legs buckled, and as she slid to her knees, Bestefar pulled her into his arms and held her up. Though she had barely known this soldier, his death seemed to embody all the losses, all the sacrifices being made across Norway. Somewhere, Henrik had a mother and father who would cry when they learned the news—*if* they ever learned of their son. Maybe he had a brother, or a sister, or even a girlfriend. "I tried—but it wasn't enough," she cried, her tears flowing into Bestefar's wool jacket. "I should have asked you to help, but . . . he's dead."

For a hurried moment, he wrapped her in his sturdy arms and whispered rapidly in her ear. "How could you have known? I've done my best to keep you unaware. Even scared off your well-meaning friend. You did what you could."

"Oh, Bestefar." She cried harder. "But we can't leave his body to rot or be found by the Gestapo."

"We can't bury him, Marit. There's no time."

"We could take his body with us and give him a proper burial."

"No. A dead body in tight quarters puts the living at risk."

He was right. Face wet with tears, Marit brushed past Bestefar. "I'll be right back."

"Marit!"

She raced past him out of the barn and into the farmhouse. Without taking off her boots, she flew upstairs and straight to the storage chest. The moment she lifted the lid, the sweet cedar filled her nose as she tore through tablecloths and runners to the soft wool of her *bunad* at the bottom. She couldn't let the Gestapo find it and burn it. She'd take it for Aunt Ingeborg's sake—for her own sake.

She flew down the stairs, stuffing the *bunad* inside her *jakke*.

In the kitchen, a meow startled her.

"Tekopp!" Marit cried. She wanted to bring the cat along, for Lars's sake. She could tuck him in her jacket to keep him quiet, and besides, even if he got loose there was nothing unusual about a cat roaming the harbor. She reached down, scooped him up, and tucked him in her *jakke* along with the *bunad*.

With a sense that hours had passed instead of seconds, Marit hurried down the stairs with her cargo, said a silent goodbye to the old farmhouse and her brave soldier, and fled.

## CHAPTER TWENTY-SIX

# The Shetland Bus

Marit caught up with Bestefar outside the barn, and without a word, they hurried toward the road, ducked low, and sped through the water-filled ditch. If they were stopped this time, there would be no second chance.

As they neared the boathouse, the gleaming eyes of headlights swung toward them from the Nazi headquarters. Bestefar grabbed her arm and pulled her with him to the soggy earth. Breathless, Marit rolled onto her back, careful not to squash Tekopp.

Lights cut a hazy path through the darkness and drew closer with the slow approach of wheels rolling over the wet road. For a moment, lights lit the air just above her nose. All she had to do was lift her hand and she would give them away. She remained motionless in the ditch's shadows, trying not to breathe.

Wind swooped down on them. Sleet stung Marit's face. Water seeped through the back of her *jakke* and sweater and iced the small of her back. Tekopp began to squirm and wiggle. Marit held him more tightly. But the tighter she gripped him, the more he dug his claws into her skin and struggled to escape.

*"Yeeoooow!"* he complained, but Marit held him harder.

The light and wheels stopped, and then the vehicle backed up in their direction.

"Let him go," Bestefar whispered fiercely.

Marit released her grip and Tekopp sprang from her coat. He bounded over her chest, his claws raking her neck as he fled.

A door opened. *"Halt! Was ist los?"* A second door opened and boot heels sounded on the road above. Another light swept back and forth.

Her heart thudded louder with each passing second.

Up on the road, a set of boots pivoted, then stopped.

The light paused in its sweeping search.

The soldier laughed, then said something more in German.

Footsteps sounded, the door shut, and wheels splattered mud as the vehicle moved slowly forward, dragging the light away with it.

A welcome darkness covered them, and their only companion was once again the wind. They held still. Silently, Marit chastised herself for trying to bring Tekopp. Finally, Bestefar stirred. In haste, they closed the remaining distance.

Aunt Ingeborg waited behind the boathouse door. "The soldier?" she whispered.

Bestefar shook his head, and Aunt Ingeborg seemed to understand.

Life vests on, they piled wordlessly into the rowboat. Bestefar rowed quietly to the trawler, and Marit hoisted herself up the rope ladder behind Aunt Ingeborg.

Once aboard, Bestefar motioned to the hold and whispered, "The rest are below?"

Aunt Ingeborg nodded.

"Good," he said. Then he pointed Marit to the wheelhouse that sheltered the steering wheel and controls. Teeth chattering, she was wet clear through and colder than she'd ever been. From the shelter of the small wheelhouse, she watched Bestefar as he secured the dinghy to the line, lifted anchor, and single-handedly hoisted a sail to half-mast.

The wind howled outside the wheelhouse and whined through its cracks. It couldn't be a worse time for leaving. Then she realized, on the contrary, maybe this was the best kind of weather. The Germans wouldn't want to be out on the water in such a storm.

As soon as the sail rose partway up the mast, the wind turned on the canvas and pressed the trawler toward the waves. Marit hung on to the handholds inside the wheelhouse as the boat tilted. Bestefar squeezed in beside her, his slicker rain-drenched.

"We can't afford to start the engine in the harbor," he whispered. "Someone could hear—even in this wind."

They skimmed out of the safety of the breakwater. When they crossed into open water, Bestefar gave her the wheel. "Keep it steady. See where the compass is? Just hold it there on course."

Then he bustled outside again, dropped the sail, and returned to join her in the wheelhouse. He throttled the engine forward. The engine caught and hummed, but out of the sheltered harbor, the wind drowned out the trawler's usual *tonk-tonk-tonk* noise.

Like a madman, the wind rocked their cradle. Rain drenched the wheelhouse windows. Now, finally, it would be safe to talk.

"I'm sorry, Bestefar," she said, certain that the wind drowned her voice to anyone onshore. "I didn't understand you. When you turned in your radio, I thought you'd given up completely."

"I lied," he said heavily. The lines and creases in his face had multiplied, and beneath his eyes, his skin was dark with worry. "I gave up the one radio, but I still have another disguised as a tackle box—here on the trawler."

"Oh, but I thought . . . I was so angry at you for—I'm sorry."

Then he explained how he'd initially intended to stay clear of getting involved. But when the Resistance came to him and asked him to fix a boat engine, he did what he could, and his involvement grew. He'd helped transport shipments of arms for the Allies and captained a boatload of agents and soldiers *into* Norway, "right under the noses of the Nazis," and this was his third trip of transporting refugees.

"So that's why you were gone so long at times."

He nodded. "And your soldier?"

In turn, she told him how she'd stumbled across Henrik, hid him, and tried to finish his mission by delivering the compass. "On the way back, that's when the wind caught us—"

"All the more reason to get you off the island. People have a way of talking, especially when under pressure by the Gestapo. This war, it changes people—and not always for the better."

Outside the wheelhouse, boat lines that should have been secured suddenly danced in the darkness like angry white snakes. "Bestefar, look!"

"Stay here," he ordered, "and keep your hands on the wheel. Keep us pointing southwest." He stepped out again into the night.

Shivering, Marit watched the compass and turned the

wheel back and forth to counter the force of waves and wind. The compass needle careened west, then south, but each time, she brought it back halfway between the two points.

Waves crested higher than the gunwales. Maybe this whole trip was a suicide trip, an escape from the Nazis only to be swallowed by the sea. Finally, Bestefar returned again, dripping wet. His wrist was chafed and bleeding.

Bestefar took the wheel. "*Takk.* Now get below with the others." He pointed to the hatch midship, which usually held a full day's catch of fish. "And hold on to something as you cross that deck!"

Blinking back blowing rain and salt water, Marit bent low and steadied herself by gripping the boom, which was now secured, its sail down. At the hatch on deck, she knocked and the square door opened.

"Quickly. Don't let in rain," Aunt Ingeborg called.

Arms caught her and directed her feet. She squeezed down alongside two bodies—Aunt Ingeborg's and Lars's—and the rest, sitting or lying down in the hold.

"I brought the *bunad.*" A chill had settled deep in her bones. Her teeth chattered and her mouth had grown stiff with cold. "I wouldn't let the Nazis have it."

She couldn't see her aunt's face, but in the few seconds of silence that followed, she knew Aunt Ingeborg was pleased. "Oh, Marit." A hand reached over—a welcome comfort of softness and calluses.

"You have so much to tell me," her aunt said. "But not now. We should try to sleep."

Silence enveloped them and the air reeked of fish. Later she would explain everything to her aunt, but for now, Marit was drenched and bitterly cold. Wedged between bodies, she closed her eyes. Eventually she warmed, and lulled by the rumbling engine, she slept.

More than once during the night the pregnant woman retched in the darkness. Someone must have found her a bucket, because the hatch opened, something clunked on deck, and then the hatch closed again. "I'm sorry," the woman said.

"No need to apologize," Aunt Ingeborg replied.

Marit tucked her nose inside her sweater, which helped only somewhat, and managed to go back to sleep. Though she didn't know the stories of the other passengers or why they were fleeing, she understood they were all in danger—and that they were drawn together as close as family in the belly of the boat.

Sometime around dawn, Marit guessed, Aunt Ingeborg woke everyone. "Listen!"

Before Marit opened her eyes, she jumped up and bumped her head.

"Everyone—stay below," Aunt Ingeborg ordered, then lifted the hatch slightly.

Through the crack, Marit glimpsed the dusky gray sky

and a low-swooping plane coming from the north. It droned closer and dropped lower until it was nearly upon them. If the boat was shot to pieces, it would become their coffin. God would have to protect them. They were only a fishing trawler alone on a vast sea—no match for Nazi bomber planes.

She and Aunt Ingeborg watched as Bestefar slipped from his wheelhouse and ducked beside an overturned wooden barrel, its lid askew. "The barrel doesn't contain herring or extra fuel oil," her aunt explained, "but guns and rifles."

"How do you know?" Marit asked.

"I know."

Droning low, the plane approached, drawing closer and closer. As it did, Bestefar reached into the barrel. But to Marit's relief, the plane turned sharply away and then flew off into the charcoal sky until it was no longer visible. The pilot must have thought they were a simple fishing boat.

"Thank God!" Aunt Ingeborg shouted. She dropped the hatch, and darkness and the damp, sharp smells of fish, fuel oil, and vomit engulfed them again.

"I can't stay down here," Marit said. She pushed open the hatch and scrambled onto the deck. "And Bestefar needs help keeping watch."

"Marit!" her aunt warned.

"I'll stay out of sight in the wheelhouse," she called over her shoulder. She didn't want to disobey her aunt, but this time Bestefar needed her.

All morning and afternoon, Marit helped Bestefar keep watch for approaching German planes. If one were to come too close and open up on them with gunfire, he'd be ready beside the gun-filled barrel. He might be able to inflict some damage in return, and Marit would keep the boat on course.

The storm had passed, settling into a steady drizzle. Winds blew across giant swells, and their mood grew more confident as they traveled southwest. When a spray of water shot into the sky, not far from their boat, Marit panicked. From her nightmares, her first reaction was— *kraken*! But she knew she wasn't being logical. It was far worse. "Submarine!" she yelled to Bestefar.

"Marit!" He laughed beside her in the wheelhouse. "Have you forgotten where you're from? Look again!"

A pod of humpback whales spouted from their air holes, then arced . . . rising, rising from the surface—one, two, three—until their mighty tails swept upward, revealing light-patterned undersides as they dived. For a time, the whales paralleled the trawler, as if keeping watch over them. All too soon, they veered away, and gulls followed in their wake.

"Marit, until we reach Scalloway, I need an extra set of eyes."

Long after sunset and late into the night, eyes straining with fatigue, Marit kept watch for planes, boats, or mines that might have drifted off course into open water. Several times, Bestefar motioned for her to go below, but she shook her head. She refused to give up her post. Bestefar couldn't navigate and keep watch for so many hours all alone.

A full twenty-four hours later, they'd covered over three hundred kilometers to Shetland, the islands off the northern tip of Scotland. Out of the vast darkness, a few lights flickered in the distance, and Bestefar steered straight for the British base in Scalloway. At his direction, Marit opened the hatch, and one by one, everyone came up on deck. The pregnant woman was pale and unsteady with sickness. Lars held fast to Aunt Ingeborg's hand.

As they entered the harbor, Bestefar slowed the engine and sounded the siren several times.

"A message in code?" Marit asked.

"Morse code," he said. "The letter *V*, for *victory*."

Like gathering fireflies, lights flickered on in the harbor. Soon, a growing crowd of men—and a few women—gathered at the wharf, waiting to greet them.

Marit stepped to the stern, gripped the rail from the back of the trawler, and gazed out.

Beyond the black ocean, her parents waited.

Her country waited.

## CHAPTER TWENTY-SEVEN

# Homecoming

*Three Years Later*

"**W**ill all the Germans be gone?" Marit asked as the fishing trawler neared the humpback island of Godøy. The city of Ålesund lay beyond, framed by mountains crowned white.

"That's our hope," Bestefar replied.

She worried, along with everyone, that with 350,000 Germans lingering on Norwegian soil, they might try for a last stand and leave the country in ruins. Over the radio, the king and Resistance leaders kept advising Norwegians not to take revenge, but to be patient—and wait.

Marit stood outside the wheelhouse, its door ajar as Bestefar steered the fishing trawler into the familiar wharf. Lars, Aunt Ingeborg, and several other passengers stood watching from the bow. Morning sunlight danced off the sea as the boat rode its gentle swells. As they passed island farms, Norwegian flags flew proudly from every flagpole. Marit breathed in the saltwater air. They were actually returning home.

When the news had come to the world—and to the village of Scalloway on Shetland—Marit was in the dining hall gathered with others around the radio. It was May 8, 1945, and Winston Churchill officially declared that peace had come at last to Europe. The room filled with cheering, then singing and dancing that went on for hours. Marit danced with Resistance soldiers, with Lars, with Aunt Ingeborg and Bestefar. She felt herself return to a semblance of who she once was: a girl without fear. But she was hardly the same. She was ten when the first bombs had fallen. Now she was fifteen.

For the last three years, thousands of refugees— including the men and women who had journeyed with them on the trawler—passed through Scalloway and on to England, the United States, and other Allied countries. Some went where they had relatives, some had no family left and decided to start over, some received special training and returned to Norway to help the Resistance. Some stayed on in Scalloway, a compact village of a thousand people, including Marit, Lars, and Aunt Ingeborg, who helped in the base's kitchen and boarded with a blind, elderly woman at a nearby farm. Bestefar made numerous trips with his trawler between Shetland and Norway's treacherous coast, and each time he returned to Scalloway, Marit hugged him fiercely. Now, with the news of peace, the German occupation of Norway—five long and bitter years—had finally come to an end!

As soon as they could ready the trawler, they once again made the long crossing. Seagulls circled the trawler, expecting scraps from a regular fishing voyage. Marit's stomach fluttered. She longed to touch shore. The engine slowed, its reassuring *tonk-tonk-tonk* reminding her that some things had not changed.

She studied the crowd, bracing herself for the sight of grayish green uniforms. But she didn't see a single German soldier anywhere. Friends cheered as their boat docked in the harbor. She could see tall Mr. Larsen, Mrs. Brottem, and a young woman with dark hair held back in a scarf who cried out, "Marit! You're back!"

"Hanna!" Marit raced across the deck and didn't wait for the plank. She squeezed under a rail and jumped onto the dock. Hanna's face was thin, and when Marit hugged her, knobby shoulders spoke of food shortages. But the slice of air between Hanna's front teeth was still the same, and her smile belied the years of hardship. "There's so much we need to talk about," Hanna said, then she turned. "Miss Halversen!"

Beyond the crowd, Marit caught sight of a new large sign on Mr. Larsen's general store that read "Closed for joy!" She smiled.

Soon after, when they neared the farm, Marit stopped abruptly. Above the door of the goldenrod farmhouse hung a red and black swastika flag. What if a few Germans remained? She couldn't move. But Bestefar didn't falter. He strode ahead, ripped down the flag, threw it to the ground, and spat on it.

Then he searched the house, chicken coop, and barn. Though the Nazis had taken over their farmhouse, they were gone now. "At least," Bestefar said, "they didn't burn everything to the ground in their retreat."

That day, Marit helped scrub every room from top to bottom. On her hands and knees Aunt Ingeborg declared, her face red from scouring, "I want every trace, every scent of them gone forever!"

Marit happily ripped down the paper that had covered the windows and blackened the landscape. Despite the long summer hours of evening light, she lit candles on every windowsill—along with the rest of the islanders. No more darkness. No more occupation.

With each day that followed, Marit waited for news of her parents. While in Scotland, they'd heard rumors from others working for the Resistance. Someone saw them arrested by the Nazis. Another said they were living in Oslo. But with no letters or messages, she could not know if they were alive or dead, and in her memory, their faces had dimmed. But from her time at the base, she'd come to better understand the workings of the Resistance. They had waged war against the Germans by slipping soldiers and ammunitions into Norway; by blowing up German ships, trains, and supply trucks; and by helping countless refugees—teachers, pastors, dislocated families, Jews and non-Jews—anyone, adults or children, escape.

One morning in late May, when raindrops fell sideways, Marit and Lars waited for the mail boat to arrive. Not only did new supplies arrive daily, but each boatload brought returning islanders—some who had escaped, others who had joined the underground militia, and still others who had simply disappeared.

In a light rain, Marit and Lars took shelter under a boathouse eave. Once the mail boat docked, a thin couple made their way down the plank. The man limped badly and used a cane, and the woman, whose hair was shorn, carried a small rucksack. They were like leafless trees, angular in form, their limbs unsteady in the breeze. But when they glanced out at the crowd, Marit recognized their eyes immediately. Her throat closed and she couldn't find her voice. She thought her heart would explode.

Finally, she screamed, "Mama! Papa!"

In a few long strides—in one fierce embrace—they were reunited. Laughing, crying, hugging, examining one another.

On their slow walk to the farmhouse, Papa explained that they needed to build up their strength before—or if—they returned to Isfjorden. Their home there had been bombed again, this time to splinters. For now, Papa would help Bestefar fish and Mama would help at the school in the fall.

"We met there for school," Lars explained, with a nod in the direction of the church. The wind caught his sandy hair, and for a second, with his growing frame, he reminded Marit of a fjord horse—sturdy and dependable. "But this fall," he continued, "the schoolhouse is ours again." He spoke as if the island had always been his home. "Aunt Ingeborg made us study while we were at Scalloway so we wouldn't fall behind. I'll be in grade six this year."

That day at the table, everyone had stories.

Mama told how she worked as a translator from their

*hytte* in the mountains. She worked alongside a Briton and a Norwegian—both radio operators. "But the British soldier," she said, shaking her head, "turned out to be German. His accent was so good he fooled even me. Many died because of him. Dozens of us were arrested."

"Papa," Lars said. "What did you do?"

Papa stirred his *kaffe* slowly, seemingly lost in his thoughts. At first Marit wondered if he'd heard Lars's question. Finally, he spoke. "I mapped out bridges, train trestles, tunnels, and highways for destruction—the very things I helped design and build, I helped blow up. We had to handicap the Nazis, whatever way we could."

Marit told about Henrik, and how she'd delivered his coded message about klipfish and his compass by rowboat with Lars, to the north side of the island.

"We'll never know for sure," Aunt Ingeborg added, "but the compass Marit delivered just might have been the same compass our host received as a signal to move us on. All I know is that we were sent from our basement shelter to take the Shetland Bus. I thought it was going to be a real bus."

In the rhubarb patch, Marit worked alongside Mama and Aunt Ingeborg, harvesting the sturdy, bittersweet red stalks. Now that the first Allied food shipments were arriving, they could count on sugar and flour, and they planned to make jams, jellies, pies, and sauces to store, sell, and trade. Since she'd returned to Godøy Island, chores had never felt so good.

As Marit pulled out the tender pink stems from the moist, rich earth, she spotted a few slimy gray slugs clinging to them. Disgusted, she flicked them off, one by one. But rhubarb was hearty. It endured droughts and heavy rains, bitter winters—and war. What were a few slugs? Before moving to the next plant with its massive green leaves, she stood up, stretched out the knot in the small of her back, and gazed toward the pasture and sea.

Papa and Lars worked at repairing the fence. Sweat marked a *V* on Papa's shirt between his jutting shoulder blades as he dropped a cedar beam into the ground. Then Lars tapped dirt around the new fence pole. She hated to think about how Papa and Mama had been held at the Grini concentration camps outside Oslo. Papa refused to discuss the treatment he was subjected to, but when they'd all gone swimming, the pale scars on his legs and back made Marit wince. Separated at a men's camp and women's camp, her parents had each done hard labor, and the food portions were, according to Mama, "never, never enough."

"Mama?" Marit asked, glancing over at her mother, who was bent over a rhubarb plant. "Do you want to take a rest?"

Mama looked up, her eyes still bright as crystal blue fjord waters. "Rest? Why would I want to rest? This is play!" She laughed, but that started up the cough that she'd brought back from the camp. Sometimes she coughed up blood. Her face, gaunt and sunken, barely resembled that of the woman who had smoothed Marit's hair and had said goodbye five years earlier at the ferry.

Her parents' work in the Resistance had come at a high price. Did they feel their efforts had been worth the sacrifice? Marit wondered. And her own efforts of delivering the compass and the klipfish code, even though her role had been small—had she made any difference at all? She remembered her aunt's words: *You must do what you feel is right, and so must I.* And so had poor Henrik, at such a terrible price. Would she do the same if she had the chance to do it all over again?

She expected so.

"I'm surprised the Germans left this rhubarb patch," Mama said between coughs. "They certainly didn't leave anything else."

"From the bottles we found in the barn," Aunt Ingeborg said, her long braid hanging over her shoulder, "they were probably drinking more than eating these last months. They must have sensed the end was coming."

The goats and chickens were gone. Only Olga

remained. Earlier, Olaf had come by to explain how he'd asked the German soldiers if he could milk Olga for them, and in return he was allowed a weekly pail of milk for his family. It was his way, he'd told Marit, to help out until Olga's real owners returned. Unfortunately, only days after their return, locals asked Olaf's parents to leave the island. They sold their home and left to start over somewhere else. Marit never had a chance to say goodbye to Olaf.

Across the pasture, no soldiers flanked the lighthouse. Only seagulls, oystercatchers, and terns frequented its nearby shore. Now that Hitler was dead and the Nazis had lost, now that Germany was in ruins, she wondered about her lighthouse soldier—the one who gave her two chocolates in exchange for her *dyne*. Did he question the teachings of Hitler and the Nazi propaganda now? How had the war changed young men like him?

Marit turned back to gathering rhubarb. The sun pressed its warmth along her bare arms. A sea breeze cooled her back and neck. Her family was together again. The war was truly over. A deep joy coursed through her from head to toes. She was only picking rhubarb behind a barn. A simple thing. She was only doing chores on a piano key of farmland off the western coast of Norway.

On Godøy Island.

She was home.

# Author's Note

My research for this book included a trip to Norway, a country rich in history, landscape, and the character of its people (some of whom I proudly call my ancestors). With my husband, Charlie, and our son, Eric, we visited several World War II museums and combed the region where this story is set. The more I learned about the Resistance efforts, the more in awe I was of the bravery of ordinary Norwegians.

The Nazi occupation of Norway lasted five years. All major events of this story are historically true.

When I asked my friend Johanne Moe about her experience growing up in Nazi-occupied Norway, she replied, "I lived in constant fear." She also told me about a bomb that was wedged under the floorboards of her house, and also how Nazi soldiers would enter the house unannounced anytime of day or night, taking what they wished, including the last piece of her mother's precious soap.

Two months after the Nazis bombed Norway on April 9, 1940, they effectively defeated the Norwegian army, which had known peace for 125 years. The Nazis attempted a "friendly" occupation, regarding Norwegians as a kindred people that should preferably be led into the fold . . . through persuasion, eventually to side with the Germans. When Nazi propaganda, however, failed to win over the hearts and minds of the Norwegian people, the Nazis resorted to harsher tactics, including house raids, interrogation, and torture by the Gestapo. As a way of coping, Norwegians resorted to humor and Resistance symbols, such as wearing red hats and paper clips. German-run concentration camps existed in Norway, too, and many Norwegians eventually were sent to these camps. Who was sent? Anyone who openly opposed the Nazi occupation or was caught helping with Resistance efforts.

Though this story focuses on life under Nazi occupation, it is important to note that throughout Europe the Jewish population was treated most severely. In Norway, the property of Jewish citizens was the first to be confiscated, and all Jewish males over the age of fifteen were sent to the brutal concentration camps in Germany, never to return. According to one author, the "Norwegian Jewish community suffered the greatest losses of all Scandinavian countries."

Despite the Nazis' terrorizing presence and demands, Norway's pastors and teachers rallied together and took bold stands. Lutheran pastors refused to stay in their churches under the new banner of Nazi authority and preach as they were instructed. Instead, most left their pulpits and took risks by meeting with church members in private homes, much as Pastor Ecklund chose to do.

When Quisling's new government passed laws to establish a Nazi teachers' association, as well as a national youth organization, similar to the Nazi Youth in Germany, both were met with great protests. The Nazi Youth organizations in Germany had been highly successful in molding young minds toward a Nazi philosophy. By making every Norwegian boy and girl between the ages of ten and eighteen attend such meetings and activities, the Nazis hoped to have similar success in Norway. The Church of Norway objected. More than 200,000 parents wrote letters refusing to allow their children to participate in the "Nazi Youth" organizations. The teachers, too, rallied together in this struggle to protect the freedoms of teachers and students. In short, when the Nazi leadership ordered teachers across Norway to instruct students in "the new spirit" of Nazi philosophy, the teachers refused.

The retaliation toward teachers was severe.

One out of every ten teachers—just like Miss Halversen —was rounded up and sent to a concentration camp. To make an example of them, the Nazis crammed five hundred of these teachers in a ship in nightmarish, slavelike conditions and shipped them sixteen hundred miles up the frigid northern coast to a concentration camp. Some did not survive the voyage.

Despite such harsh tactics against teachers, the teachers who remained behind stood firm and refused to give in to the Nazis' demands. Eventually, the Nazi leadership relented and said the teachers had "misunderstood" their earlier demands. Though I do not know of any individual teachers who escaped en route to the camps or from them, it is certainly plausible that a teacher such as Miss Halversen might have been helped by the Resistance. In the end, the teachers won this battle against the Nazis and were left to teach according to their conscience.

Roughly 50,000 Norwegians were arrested by Nazis during the occupation. Of these, some 9,000 were sent to Nazi concentration camps in Norway that offered woeful living conditions: lack of decent food and drinking water, and hard labor. Some died and many became sick. About 9,000 Norwegians were sent to German concentration camps in Czechoslovakia, Poland, Austria, France, and Germany, where conditions were inhuman. Fourteen hundred Norwegians died at these camps—half of them of Jewish ancestry, and of these, most perished in gas chambers.

"The Shetland Bus" was the term used to describe the efforts of fishermen and boat captains who ferried refugees *out* of the country. The term "refugee" could have included almost anyone fleeing for safety: families whose homes might have been bombed in a Nazi reprisal, individuals suspected of aiding the Allies, Jews and non-Jews, or anyone who went against the Germans in any way. The bus also helped bring Allied weapons, supplies, and agents *into* Norway. Scotland's Shetland Islands lay roughly two hundred miles away from the middle of Norway's western coast, and boats traveled these waters at great risk in the dark arctic months. Ålesund and its surrounding islands, including Godøy, harbored numerous Shetland Bus operations.

Some 3,300 people escaped from Norway via small boats—with heavy losses—and close to 50,000 people crossed the border on foot, largely into Sweden.

After five bitter years of German occupation in Norway, Winston Churchill declared over British radio that peace had come at last to Europe. On May 8, 1945, bells rang out joyously across Norway. The Norwegian flag shot up every flagpole. Radios came out of hiding. On May 17, children marched throughout Norway in their annual Children's Parade on Independence Day, which had been banned since the occupation. Finally, on June 7, fireworks filled the sky as Norwegians celebrated their greatest symbol of freedom—the long-awaited return of their exiled king.

# GLOSSARY

## Norwegian Words:

**alt for Norge** (ahlt forr nor-geh) all for Norway

**Bestemor** (behss-tah-moor) Grandmother

**Bestefar** (behss-tah-faar) Grandfather

**bunad** (boo-nahd) traditional costume of Norway, consisting of blouse, vest, and skirt for women and girls; and shirt, vest, and knickers for men and boys

**dyne** (dee-nah) a down-filled quilt, or eiderdown filled duvet

**fattigmann** (faht-tih-mahn) twisted and fried dough flavored with cinnamon and cardamon seed

**frokost** (froo-kost) breakfast

**God Jul** (goo-yewl) Merry Christmas

**god morgen** (goo-maw-ern) good morning

**god natt** (goo-nahtt) good night

**hei** (hay) a greeting; hey there

**hytte** (hit-ah) cabin

**ja** (ya) yes

**jakke** (yak-keh) jacket or coat

**jøssing** (yuhs-sing) a Norwegian patriot

**Julaften** (yewleh-ahf-tern) Christmas Eve

**Juletid** (yewleh-teed) Christmastime

**kaffe** (kahf-feh) coffee

**Kaptain** (kahp-tayn) captain

**klippfisk** (klip-fisk) klipfish; split, salted, and dried cod

**kraken** (krah-ken) a sea monster of Norwegian folklore, an enormous octopus/crab creature said to pull ships down with its tentacles

**krumkake** (kroom-kah-keh) a cone-shaped cookie baked on an iron, similar to a waffle iron

**lefse** (lef-sah) a thin potato pancake

**lutefisk** (loo-teh-fisk) a type of dish made from air-dried whitefish, prepared with lye, soaked many hours, and served with butter

**Marit** (Mahr-it) a first name

**Mor** (moor) Mother

**Nasjonal Samling (NS)** (nah-shoo-naal sahm-ling) national gathering; or Norwegian Nazi Party

**nei** (nay) no

**nisselue** (nissah-luah) red stocking cap

**Norge** (nor-geh) Norway

**pensum** (pen-summ) syllabus of classwork

**quisling** (quiz-ling) a traitor; a term used for Norwegians who collaborated with the Nazis, so named because of Vidkun Quisling, a Norwegian who worked with Nazis during the occupation

**risengrot** (rees-ehn-gruht) warm rice pudding sprinkled with cinnamon and sugar

**sandkaker** (sahn-kaa-ker) almond cookies in fluted tins

**sølje** (suhl-yeh) type of Norwegian silver broach

**takk** (tahkk) thank you

**tekopp** (teh-kopp) teacup

**tusen takk** (two-sehn tahkk) a thousand thanks, or many thanks

**uff da** (oohf-dah) an exclamation of dismay

**vaffel** (vahff-ell) waffle

**vel** (vehl) *well!*

**velkommen** (vehl-kom-mehn) Welcome

**vesla** (vehs-lah) "little one"

## Norwegian Places:

**Ålesund** (ohleh-sunn) city on the western coast of Norway

**Alnes** (ahl-nes) fishing village on the north of Godøy Island

**Åndalnes** (ohn-dahl-nes) a city at the end of Romsdal Fjord in west-central Norway

**Giske** (gih-skeh) an island off Norway's western coast near Ålesund

**Godøy** (goo-dey) an island off Norway's western coast near Ålesund

**Isfjorden** (ees-fjorh-ehn) a village at the end of Romsdal Fjord

## German Words:

**Fräulein** (froy-leyen, or froy-line) girl; miss

**Gestapo** (Geh-stah-poh) Germany's secret police

**Halt! Was ist los?** (Halt, pronounced as in English; Vahs ist lohs) Stop! What's the matter?

**Heil** (heyel, or hile) Hail

**Herr** (hehrr) man; mister

**Reich** (rahyk) empire; German Nazi state

**Was ist das?** (Vahs ist dahs) What is that?

# For Further Reading

*Folklore Fights the Nazis: Humor in Occupied Norway*
by Kathleen Stokker
Madison: University of Wisconsin Press, 1995

*Norway 1940*
by François Kersaudy
New York: St. Martin's Press, 1990

*Norway 1940–45: The Resistance Movement*
by Olav Riste and Berit Nokleby
Oslo: Tanum-Norli, 1970

*The Shetland Bus*
by David Howarth
New York: Lyons Press, 1951

*Snow Treasure*
by Marie McSwigan
New York: E. P. Dutton, 1942

*War and Innocence:*
*A Young Girl's Life in Occupied Norway*
by Hanna Aasvik Helmersen
Seattle: Hara Publishing, 2000

⟶ ❁ ⟵

AVON PUBLIC LIBRARY
BOX 977/200 BENCHMARK RD.
AVON, CO 81620